MUSIC CAN BE MURDER

Pearl R Meaker

Copyright © 2018 Pearl R Meaker
All rights reserved

This is a work of fiction. Characters, places, and events are the product of the author's imagination or are used fictitiously. Any resemblance to real people, companies, institutions, organizations or incidents is entirely coincidental, or used with their permission.

"There's a need for murder in every culture."
Mitch Jayne
1928 – 2010
Front man and bass player for the bluegrass band
The Dillards

CHAPTER 1

"Summer time . . . and the livin' is ee-zz-yy."

I did a sideways slide from the fridge to the counter by the toaster oven as I belted out the lyrics to "Summertime" from the old Gershwin opera *Porgy and Bess*.

"Fish are jumpin', don't you know, and the cotton is high-eye. Your daddy's rich . . ."

Fat chance on that one. Neither my daddy nor my husband was rich. I took four slices of diet multigrain bread out of the wrapper and arranged them on the rack, pushed it in, and shut the oven door.

". . . and your mama's good loo-oo-kin'."

They got that part right, I thought before my self-conscious subconscious reminded me that I'm not all that good-looking. I bent down, checked my reflection in the toaster oven door, and decided I wasn't that bad either. Darkish-reddish brunette hair with a hint of grey, warm brown eyes, a face others have said is pretty, five foot five, and pudgy. That's pretty much the whole package.

I turned to the coffee maker and pushed its *on* button, when a noise made me spin around. There he stood—the love of my life, Dr. Jebbin Crawford.

"'Mornin', Emory," he mumbled. He's not a morning person.

We make a cute couple, or so we've been told. He's a bit Paul Bunyan-like at six feet tall and husky. His thick, wavy, black hair brushes the top of his collar in the back, flops onto his forehead in the front, and is sprinkled all over with gray, as is his short-cropped beard. Like me, he's not as firm as he used to be. He's much more a squishy Teddy bear-type than a rough-living lumberjack. He's all mine and I'm the luckiest woman anywhere because he is.

I needed to finish my song, so I sauntered over to Jebbin, placing my index finger in front of my lips.

"So hush, my handsome baby." Another change of lyric, but hey, he's not a "little" baby. "Do-on't you cry-eye!"

A kiss on his lips finished my performance.

"Mmm! Nice kiss," he whispered into my ear as we hugged.

I pulled back to look up at him. "That was the best way I could think of to keep the baby from crying." I tapped him on the nose, then went back to the counter to start scrambling the eggs I'd already cracked into a bowl.

"Are you off to school right after you eat?" I asked without looking back at him.

"Yep. I have that report for the dean to finish up and some things to do in the lab."

Jebbin came up behind me, checking to see if there was enough coffee in the pot to pour a cup. There was. I heard him take his "Chemists do it periodically on the table" mug out of the dish drainer, fill it, then sit at his place at the table.

"A report for the dean." I laughed. "And the students think they're the only ones with dreaded reports to write."

I poured the eggs into the pan, added pieces of deli ham and American cheese, and then turned on the gas burner before setting the dial on the toaster oven.

"At least I don't have to grade this one. I'd rather write than grade." Jebbin laughed.

His first cup of coffee was gone and he got up to get more. As usual, he'd downed the first so fast I wondered why he bothered to sit down instead of just tossing it back while standing by the coffee maker.

"Tom gets all the fun of poring over it and wondering how to present it to the Board of Trustees. We humble department heads are usually spared from going into the inner sanctum. A good thing, since I have to deal with college politics more than I like already." He sat back down. "It's a part of being a professor that no one warns you about when you're so pie-in-the-sky excited to land that coveted first teaching position."

His first teaching position had been his only teaching position. He was hired for a semester when a chemistry prof went on a sabbatical, which had been a job search in disguise. Twombly College liked Jebbin's work, and we liked Twombly College. They offered the position to Jebbin, he accepted their offer, and we're still here twenty-three years later.

"Emory?"

There was a pause, so I looked up from stirring the eggs in the pan.

He was looking at me with his brows drawn together. "You sure you're OK with Molly going to Europe for that summer art history course?"

My shoulders tightened. "Yes, I'm fine with it."

I turned back to the eggs. He didn't need to see me tearing up. Lanthan, our son, and his wife, Felysse, live in Illinois, but not very close to us. Far enough for a one-day trip to be too hectic, and their schedules don't leave much room for longer trips. I miss them dearly, and I'm still learning how to cope with not seeing them more often. But Molly and I are real close, best friends close, and it was going to be hard not having our youngest nearby. After the summer in Europe, she would be starting her masters in art history at the University of Illinois in Urbana, a couple of hours drive away.

I smiled as I thought of them. Smiled at their names as I often do. Their names are short for what's on their birth certificates. Lanthanum (symbol La, atomic number 57) David Leon Crawford, and Molybdenum (symbol Mo, atomic number 42) Helen

Crawford. Elements. Perfect for a chemistry professor's kids, and really, normal enough sounding names once you shorten them.

Thinking about their names lightened my mood somewhat, though I was still thin-skinned about Molly being gone. "It's a wonderful opportunity for her. If Mom hadn't passed away before the nursing home got all her money, we couldn't have swung it." My voice was quavering.

"Yep, it is that. What's on your agenda for today?" He adroitly changed the subject.

I took a deep breath and let it out slowly. "I'll be doing PR work for the college this morning." I got the tremor under control. "Manning our information table where the conferees to the Midwest Anthropological Studies Society will be registering. Then I'm in the library this afternoon."

The toaster oven dinged. I turned down the flame under the eggs to take care of the toast. My shoulders relaxed as I spread peanut butter on the slices.

"They're updating the paranormal section, seeing as Chuck Staunton is offering courses in it now. I might find some interesting reading while I'm cataloging and shelving. I might even take a class on it." I turned and winked at my good man. "Maybe I'll learn how to bewitch you."

"You already have." One bright blue eye winked back from behind his glasses.

"I had to get you before anyone else did."

I gave Jebbin a kiss on the thinning spot at the back of his head as I set his plate in front of him, then sat down across from him and reached for the pepper. "I'll also be straightening up the anthropology section. Those classes sure picked up after Archie's book became such a hit. I really should read it. I'm sure he'll be more full of himself than usual now."

I tasted my eggs. Nope, they needed more pepper. Two more twists from the pepper mill should do it.

"Yes, he probably will. Archie's a good egg though. Don't forget we're doing that gig with him for the entertainment after the anthropologists' big dinner tonight."

"Oops! How did I manage to forget that?" I remembered the gig but not that it was tonight. "Thanks for reminding me. He's a good egg, all right, but with that ego of his, he's an ostrich egg."

Jebbin laughed. "Yeah, yeah. Big egos are a fiddle player thing."

I play fiddle too, so was perfectly within my rights when I stuck out my tongue. He was just feeling out numbered. He'd be the only part of the trio not playing fiddle. But then, bluegrass sounds better with a banjo or guitar, and Jebbin plays both.

"Do you still have the playlist he sent? Archibald wants those murder songs in top form since they fit in with his book." He ignored my childish gesture.

"Yes, I have the list. At least he mixed it up with other songs. Nothing but murder songs would make for depressing after-dinner music."

"Too true." Jebbin agreed, as the conversation then turned to other matters while we finished up our breakfast.

I breathed deeply and smiled as I walked to Blythe Hall to be the face of Twombly College, greeting the people attending the Midwest Anthropological Studies Society's conference. Twombly College's campus is a joy. Old Jairus Aiden Merriweather Twombly the First surely did things in a big way when he built the college. Trees of many different indigenous species shade much of the area. Sidewalks and paths crisscross the lawns, taking walkers and bicyclists throughout the campus. Several types and styles of gardens offer areas to rest, relax, meditate, draw, paint, or take photos. And everything draws your attention to the main building, Blythe Hall.

At two city blocks long, the Hall looks like a building from an old English university with its slate roof, mullioned windows, and turreted central tower. Its two floors at one time housed the entire college, but now it holds administrative offices, four large meeting rooms, the performing arts department classrooms, and the large ornate auditorium that was part of the original layout of the building. It also includes the library, which has expanded over the years to encompass the entire second floor.

There weren't many cars in the lot to the south of the Hall. Things slow down on campus for the first couple of weeks in June. Summer term doesn't start until mid-month. Staff and faculty take vacations or are just plain lax about early mornings until classes start. Plus, it was Friday, and professors in particular tend to include summer Fridays as part of the weekend.

I heard someone beep-locking their car. A slender man with conservatively cut, light brown hair left a dark green Mini Cooper and walked toward the Hall's main entrance. He arrived at the huge main doors as I started up the three shallow steps leading to them. He saw me coming and held the door open.

"A gentleman!" I smiled cheerfully. "I thought that was frowned upon in these enlightened times."

"All the more reason to do it." He winked and chuckled. He looked like the stereotypical academic: sporting loafers and khaki pants, with a solid, pale-yellow polo shirt, (which did nothing for his pale complexion). He even squinted through tortoiseshell-rimmed glasses.

"Thank you. Are you here for the Midwest Anthropologic Studies Society's conference?" I was beginning to wish the group had a shorter name.

"I am indeed." He beamed at me. "Are you?"

"No, I'm a local." I walked through the door he held open. "My husband is on the faculty here at Twombly. Dr. Jebbin Crawford, chemistry." I offered him my hand. "I'm Emory Crawford."

"Dr. Timothy Law." His voice was deep for how thin he was, his smile charming, and his grip was firm without hurting.

"I'll show you to the registration table, Dr. Law."

We walked through the foyer lined with marble busts of famous academics and the school seal set into the tiles of the floor.

"I'm headed that way anyway. I'm taking care of the college's information table this morning. I often do when we have conferences on campus. It's so much fun to see all the different people and learn a bit about what they do."

He trailed just behind me as we turned right into the main hallway. The registration and information tables were a few yards down the hall.

"You should stop by the library while you're here." I gestured to the large main staircase going up on our left. "We have a large anthropology section and we put up a nice display on the subject especially for the conference."

"You're a librarian?"

"No." I shook my head. "Volunteer."

We'd arrived at the tables. The Midwest Anthropological Studies Society's welcome banner stretched across the fronts of two tables pushed together end to end. The usual selection of name badges, handout packets, canvas carry bags with the MASS logo on them, and various cheap promotional doodads covered the tables in tidy rows. Off to the right was our information table with a Twombly College banner stretched across it and school promotional trinkets neatly arranged on top.

A cheerful-looking older woman sat squarely at the middle of the MASS tables. She looked old enough to be something her colleagues might study with her pure white hair wound into a bun and held with hair-sticks, an amply lined and wrinkled face, and a matronly build beneath a daintily patterned cotton blouse. I noticed that her pale blue eyes glittered with recognition as Dr. Law approached the table, so I turned my attention to Twombly's table to leave them to their greetings. Well, at least my eyes were on my table. My ears weren't.

"Hello, Myra," Dr. Law said warmly. "Good to see you here taking care of registrations, as always."

"Hello, Timothy, it's good to see you too. Where else would I be?" She chuckled. "This is the best place to find out everything about everyone who's attending. And you know me, I have to be in the know."

I glanced over, caught her self-satisfied expression, then moved behind my table and sat down. Despite her extra weight, she exuded an aura of peppy energy.

"How're things over at McGarvey College?" I heard her ask.

"Slow. It's summer break." They both laughed at the joke. "Are you still chasing after all those Amish gents of yours?"

He sounded like an annoying little brother, and she giggled like a schoolgirl.

"You tease! They aren't Amish, they just look like it to the unobservant. They're Hutterites, and I don't think any of them would like an atheist for a wife." She paused. "I hear McGarvey's cutting your department's budget."

"Rumors, Myra, nothing but nasty rumors." The earlier warmth left Dr. Law's voice.

I pretended to look at one of the brochures at my table while peeking over it to watch the two at the other table. Myra didn't look ornery, but she was certainly making Dr. Law uncomfortable. Red was creeping up his neck as he stuffed things into one of the canvas totes.

"Word's out that you were told to get a book written, one like Archie's that's a public success. Or they'll find a new department head."

"That's news to me, Myra. Where's the dorm we're staying in?" He obviously wanted to change the subject.

"James A. Oglethorpe Residence Hall is the first building to the north of this building." Falling for his ploy Myra handed him one of the campus maps on her table. She poked it with a pudgy forefinger.

"You are here. Oglethorpe is there. The parking lot is on the north side of the dorm, so past the building." She held the map out towards him. "Here, take it. I've got plenty. Pick up your keys at the service desk in the lobby of the dorm. Do you have someone rooming with you, Timothy?"

"No, I have a single, Myra." He twitched the map from her fingers." And I will now be on my way."

I looked up as he approached my table.

"Nice meeting you . . . Emily was it?" This time he held his hand out to me first.

I smiled and shook it. "Emory, after the university in Georgia, and it was nice meeting you, too, Dr. Law. Don't forget to check out the library sometime during the week."

"I won't. I may see you there later, Emory."

Just after he disappeared around the corner into the foyer, I heard a loud, familiar voice greeting Dr. Law by first name. Timothy's reply was unintelligible, but his tone did not match the other's enthusiasm. Moments later, a man and woman came around the corner. I had the voice right. Dr. Archibald Finlay Dawson, whom Jebbin and I know from jams at bluegrass festivals, was at the registration tables in a couple of strides—along with a perky-looking young lady. Currently he is anthropology's biggest shining star since Margaret Mead, and he looked the part. Archie's a tall, broad, former football player whose resonant voice and size seem to fill any room he's in. I ducked behind the stand-up poster with smiling Twombly College students on it. Archibald is an all right guy, I guess, but he's more Jebbin's friend than mine, and I didn't really want to talk to him.

"Myra!" Archie's voice echoed down the long hallway. "Myra, my MASS conference sweetheart. How are you?"

"Sweet of you to say, as always, Archie dear, but it's hard to be your conference sweetheart when you always have another woman with you. And how is your wife these days?"

"Sonya's home ill again. I'll let her know you asked after her. At any rate, women make everything better, Myra, you know that." He laughed heartily. "Oh!" He caught his breath. "Oh, you do know how to charm us men. And, while we're talking about charming women, let me introduce my teaching assistant, Ms. Naomi Malkoff."

I peeked around the stand-up poster as he wrapped a muscular arm around the shoulders of the tan and fit young lady standing beside him. She didn't seem entirely comfortable with the gesture, but she didn't move away either.

"Naomi, this is Myra Fordyce, the heart and soul of our annual conferences. She's always at the registration table to make us feel welcome . . . and to see whom we're with."

Myra was beaming. "True. Very true." She didn't let Naomi get a word in edgewise. "I must know who's who and with whom and everything else one can learn when you're the first person people see at the conference." She handed the young lady her badge. "Welcome, Naomi, I hope you enjoy your first conference with us."

"Thank you, Ms. Fordyce. It's so wonderful to be here with Dr. Dawson." Naomi was a gusher. Everything about her screamed CHEERLEADER.

"Of course it is, dear." Myra turned back to Archie. "Here you go, *Dr. Dawson.* I loved your book and I'm looking forward to hearing you speak about it."

"I'm sure you are, I'm the best speaker in the society." Archie puffed himself up.

Myra shoved a map at him, pointed out Oglethorpe Hall, and after a few more self-promotional comments from Archie, the pair left.

"Pompous ass."

I heard Myra's mutter and stifled my own giggle. It was exactly what I was thinking.

"He really is the most arrogant man I know."

The voice made Myra and I both jump. I knocked over the stand-up poster, felt myself blushing as I picked it up, made some apologetic noises, and then busied myself arranging the already tidy items on the Twombly College table.

"Sorry, ma'am. I didn't mean to startle you."

I looked at the woman. Straight, shoulder-length brown hair framed a pleasant face that showed genuine concern. I glanced at her feet. Birkenstocks peeked from beneath her long, moss-green shift dress. No wonder she'd snuck up on us.

"No problem. Welcome to Twombly College." I smiled. "We hope you enjoy your visit to our campus."

"Thank you." She smiled in return before turning to Ms. Fordyce at the registration table. I sat down and watched them over the top of another brochure.

"Arrogant barely scratches the surface of Archibald Finlay Dawson, Cameron." Myra lowered her voice just a bit. "He's arrogant to the point that he never notices how many people hate him."

"People don't hate him." The younger lady tucked a wisp of hair behind her ear. "They envy him."

"I'm not so sure there's a difference between the two, Cam."

Cameron chuckled. "Well, they can produce similar results." Her voice was lilting, like delicate mezzo-soprano wind chimes.

"How was your year at Maize State?" Myra asked while Cameron filled a canvas tote in an orderly fashion.

"Predictable. How was yours at . . . weren't you at Abernathy this year?"

"I was only on campus fall semester. You know me, can't stand being cooped up anywhere for too long. In January, I left for the Schmiedeleut Hutterite colony west of Grand Forks, North Dakota."

"I keep thinking you study the Amish, Myra. They're so similar. January's a lovely time to be in North Dakota." Cameron made a face as she clipped on her ID badge.

"Now, now, my dear. It's not as if Iowa is balmy in the winter." Myra laughed at her own jest. "It was lovely in a cold, white, and gray way. And seeing my dear Hutterite friends more than makes up for the frigid temperatures."

There was a long pause and I looked up.

"Is there something wrong, dear?" Concern creased Myra's brow. "You've turned a bit pale."

Cameron was staring at the large flower arrangement centered on the right-hand table. I had noticed it earlier. It wasn't the usual florist mix of carnations and gladiolus, but rather was a huge vase of wildflowers, some of which were artificial, and herbs. I recognized the airy white heads of anise flowers and Queen Anne's lace, and the yellow ones of fennel, marigolds and, oddly enough for early summer, holly leaves and berries. There were others I wasn't sure of.

"This arrangement, did you bring it, Myra?" Cameron whispered.

Myra hefted herself off her chair to get a closer look at the large bouquet.

"Lands no, girl! It was already on the table when I got here to set up. I brought a dried flower arrangement that is much smaller and rather bedraggled looking." The heavy, older woman reached awkwardly under the table, held up a droopy flower arrangement in a cheap basket, and then stuck it back under the table. "I thought this one was prettier, so I left it." She looked back at Cameron. "Why? What's the matter?"

"I'm not sure about all of them . . ." Cameron paused, taking a breath to gather her composure. "I don't know them all, but some I recognize from my work with Revolutionary War era folk tradition. They're plants that have to do with the devil. Well," she hastened to add, "for keeping the devil and evil away, if I'm remembering correctly that is."

Myra's eyebrows went up. "Oh! Oh my! Well at least they're for keeping him away instead of inviting him to pay a visit."

"True! You're right about that, Myra. It could have been made of the sorts of plants that represent him." She leaned in for a closer look. "Still . . . it's odd that someone put it on our registration table. Hope they aren't saying we need that sort of protection." Cameron looked relieved.

"At least I don't believe in such things. God or the devil and all that." Myra shivered, making her statement less convincing. "But I think I'll send a text to a few of my Hutterite friends. They are avid prayers and I do think that positive energy is a helpful thing. Everything connects to everything, so to speak." She plopped back down in her chair at the middle of the tables.

"Send a text?" Cameron looked surprised. "I thought they weren't into phones, let alone cell phones."

"The Schmiedeleut are into technology. They have computers and everything . . . well, tightly controlled, and they still don't have televisions, but there is a lot they've embraced."

"Who'd have thought it?" Cameron grinned, shook her head, picked up the rest of her conference goodies, and shoved them into the tote. "Well, I'll be on my way. Oglethorpe dorm, right?"

Myra nodded.

"Okay. You make sure you text your friends. Some positive energy would be a good thing, and prayer is positive energy."

I believe that too, and said a short prayer of my own. The bouquet was giving me that feeling I often get before something goes wrong. The odd shiver up the spine, like something's run over my grave. Both my grannies used phrases like that for the odd shiver that sometimes crawls up one's back, settin' spine and skin to feelin' prickly and sometimes making your whole body twitch. To them, it was a part of "gettin' a knowin'" about something. A whisper in their soul about somethin' a comin', be it good or ill. I tamped it down like I always did when the whisper of "a knowin'" would try to sneak its way into me.

"I'm calling right now, dear. See you at dinner. Where is that dratted phone! You should just carry a smaller purse, Myra Fordyce." Myra spoke into the depths of her large purse as she dug around for her cell phone.

CHAPTER 2

Later that day, Archie grabbed Jebbin and me as we walked into the large meeting room where the opening dinner for the conference would soon start. Round, white-draped tables accented with the Twombly College colors of green and gold filled the middle third of the room. A small, low stage at one side and two long buffet tables on the other side took up the rest of the space. Tantalizing aromas wafted from the buffet. Archie hustled us to his table—a round table like the others but set front and center before the dais—and introduced everyone. Ms. Myra Fordyce, whom I'd met this morning, was the current MASS secretary. Next to her was Dr. Sam Johnston, the group's treasurer and vice president, followed by the society's president, Dr. Charles A. Lindbergh and his wife, Susan.

Yes, it's the poor man's real name. What are some parents thinking when they name their children? Then again, we named our two children after elements, so I'm not sure I've much room to talk. At least, we were told, the "A" stood for "Allen" instead of "Augustus." But still . . .

I moved to sit next to Myra. We had talked a little that morning when neither of us was busy with conferees arriving. I wanted to find out more about her time with the Hutterites.

"No, no, Emory!"

Archibald took hold of my shoulders, moved me over one chair, and then guided Naomi to the seat between Myra and me.

"I've been telling Naomi all about you and Jebbin and she's dying to get to know you."

Cheerleader Naomi blushed as Archie pulled her chair out for her. He did the same for me, and then sat in the chair on my right. He motioned for Jebbin to sit between him and Dr. Lindbergh.

"There you go, Jebbin. You can explain all about bluegrass music to the MASS president. Then maybe he'll get more out of my talk and our performance later." Archie smirked at the man. "And he just loves being asked about his name."

Dr. Lindbergh's discomfort at the teasing was quite obvious. "Of course." He shook Jebbin's hand. "Dr. Dawson has been talking about you, Dr. Crawford, and I'm interested in hearing how a chemist came to be interested in bluegrass music."

I envied Jebbin. He was all set for enthusiastic conversation over dinner, but I had no idea what to talk to Naomi about. Archie was easy—you just listen to him talk about himself.

Soon, we were in line at the buffet tables. Gastronomic heaven! The college's chef, Fiorello, had presented us with scrumptious options. I took one of the small chicken cordon bleu and a dainty filet mignon along with a spoonful of his excellent lentil and Swiss cheese vegetarian casserole. My salad plate got the mixed greens with diced mango and sesame-honey vinaigrette dressing, while Jebbin took a lettuce wedge with ranch dressing. Saffron wild rice, au gratin potatoes, sliced ginger carrots with slivered almonds, green beans, and mixed vegetables completed the main course selections. As always, a basket with several mini loaves of Fiorello's famous homemade whole grain bread sat on each table with whipped butter in a cut glass dish for passing around.

During the meal, I found out there was more to Naomi than I had expected and berated myself for being suckered into making assumptions based on a stereotype. She was a cheerleader, or had been, from junior high school through her undergraduate years, but there was more to her than pompoms and cheerleader's briefs.

"I really won't have time for cheerleading now." She was perky when I asked about it. "Which is fine. I'm ready to be the more studious Naomi who's working on her masters." She explained she had been a history major, but Dr. Dawson had convinced her to go into anthropology instead, so that she could get a stipend for being his teaching assistant.

"So, I did. I play cello and love chamber music, so ethnomusicology is starting to look like a good field to go into. Interest in it will surely pick up now that Dr. Dawson's book is so popular."

Cello? Chamber music? History major? As I said, so much for stereotypes.

Archie looked up at the mention of his book. "Speaking of which, do you have it with you, Naomi?"

"Oh yes! I forgot." She easily folded in half to dig into her MASS canvas tote. "Here." She held the book out for me to take.

"Personally signed to you and Jebbin." Archie made sure he was loud enough for everyone at the table to hear him. They all looked at me.

"Ah, thank you, Archie."

"What'd he write?" Myra asked me.

I opened the cover. "To my dear friends, Dr. Jebbin & Emory Crawford. Even a banjo picker should be able to understand this. Ha ha. May none of your murder songs come true! Dr. Archibald Finlay Dawson." I closed the cover. "Well, I guess I can return the one I checked out of the library this afternoon. We were planning on buying one at your signing table anyway, Archibald. Can't pass up having a signed best seller for a new doorstop."

Archie raised his eyebrows.

"I'm joshin' ya, Archie. Just joshin'."

Archie looked relieved. He laughed it off and we all went back to our own meals and conversations.

I tried not to burp out loud as we all sat around filling up the corners, as J. R. R. Tolkien's hobbits would say, at the end of our superb meal. My hopes for a little more of the dark chocolate-cherry cake, with real cherries in it, topped with real whipped cream were dashed as Jebbin licked the last moist crumbs of his piece off his fork. Naomi made yummy noises over her berry-yogurt parfait, while I could barely draw a breath to let out my contented sigh. How was I ever going to sing later?

It didn't turn out to be a concern. I had lots of time for dinner to settle.

At organizational conferences, as opposed to subject-centric ones, dinner is usually followed by the annual business meeting. The murmur of conversations ended as Dr. Lindbergh took the stage to call the meeting to order, and the student waitstaff finished clearing plates and pouring coffee. After the meeting, the keynote speaker—Dr. Archibald Finlay Dawson—would have his turn. Archie loved to hear himself talk, assuring us of at least forty-five minutes (or more) of sitting. The evening's entertainment—Archie, Jebbin and I—were to follow that.

I was getting fidgety. Who decided it's rude to knit or crochet while listening to a speaker? Unlike a lecture or a sermon, I couldn't even use the pretense of taking notes so I could doodle.

I entertained myself with looking around the room at the people at other tables. Dr. Timothy Law, my acquaintance from this morning, was at a table in the second row behind ours, along with Dr. Cameron Garrow, the lady who got spooked by the flower arrangement. Dr. Law caught me looking and gave me a nod and a smile. At a table in the back row I spotted Jairus Aiden Merriweather Twombly VI (Jam to family and close friends) and his wife Amy. The current head of the Twombly dynasty was, like all those before him, deeply involved in the college, town, and county his great-great-great-grandfather had settled and founded. He's the chairman of the college board of directors and quietly shows up when there are dinners at the school. Jairus smiled, Amy waved. I returned their greetings, then continued to look around.

I didn't see anyone else I recognized, so I grabbed one of the little pads of square paper bearing the Twombly College crest that sat by each place on the table. Tearing off a sheet, I began an origami figure. In the time it took me to make seven cranes, three bookmarks, and a butterfly that I designed myself, Dr. Lindbergh brought the business meeting to a close and announced a short break before "our best-selling author takes the podium."

Time to join the mass migration of females to the ladies room. I wondered if any sociologists had ever studied the phenomenon: "Restroom use by women at large gatherings." Men never seem to swarm theirs like we do ours.

I stared at the floor while listening to the conversations around me, not wanting to look into the mirrored walls that made up opposing sides of the restroom's lounge. The infinity effect of mirrors reflecting mirrors makes me nervous.

"I wonder how long Dr. Dawson will talk?" someone behind me spoke. "The way he dominates most conversations, I'm sure he'll go over time."

"He does seem to love hearing himself talk." Several ladies laughed.

Someone nudged me in the back even though the line hadn't moved. I looked around enough to see it was Myra.

"Your conversation with Naomi during dinner made me realize that I didn't ask you much about yourself this morning. You got me talking about my work and off I went. Rude of me, so I wanted to apologize. What do you do, Emory?"

I turned so I could focus on her face instead of looking at her shoes or the mirrors.

There it was; my least favorite question. "I'm a homemaker. A wife, mother and homemaker."

"Oh." Her eyebrows rose. "But I thought you mentioned that your children are grown. Are you returning to your career now that they are on their own?"

Steady, girl, steady, I coached myself. Don't sound defensive, snotty, or whiney. "I never had another career." I managed what I hoped was a serene smile. "I intended to, when I graduated high school, but it didn't pan out for me. I was going to leave college anyway when I met Jebbin. We married rather quickly, and I never looked into a career."

"Oh!" She was starting to get that look, the one people get when addressing a pathetic child, or just before they pat a bedraggled puppy on the head. "You don't have a degree then?"

"I got a bachelors of general studies from Twombly. Spouses can attend for free. I took classes in so many things that Jebbin looked it over and saw I'd done sufficient work and urged me to formally take the degree. But I've ... well, ah ... just never bothered to do anything with it." I tweaked my slipping smile back in place. "I'm happy being at home with my family, my hobbies, taking classes, and volunteering at the college library."

Myra fidgeted. "Oh. Well. How very nice if that's what you want. Rather like my Hutterite friends, I suppose. The women mostly say they're content with keeping house, tending family, raising vegetables, and quilting, knitting, sewing, and crocheting."

Why does this always make me feel so pathetic? But fortunately, the matter didn't go any further.

"Oh my god!" Myra hissed, grabbing my arm and looking at the mirrored wall across from us. "Sonya's here!"

"Sonya?" My brain whirred for a moment. "Archie's wife?"

"Oh my god, yes!" She leaned closer to my ear. "She hasn't been to a conference in years."

"I thought you don't believe in God, Myra. That said, which one is she?"

"I don't." She gave me a perplexed look. "It's just what everyone says when they're shocked. She's seven ladies behind me, dark hair, wearing a pale green and pink floral dress."

Sonya didn't share her husband's love of bluegrass, and since it was from festivals that we knew Archie, Jebbin and I had never met her. However, Archie had spoken of her from time to time.

I braved the look into the vast mirrored wall. Fighting vertigo and angst from the infinity of reflections, I managed to spot the tall slender woman Myra had described standing in the line. Her posture was tense, with her arms wrapped around herself—all closed in and defensive. She stared off into space, speaking to no one.

"I don't think Archibald knows she's here," Myra continued to whisper. "There will be fireworks for sure when he finds out after that story he told me about her being home sick. Not that I believed it anyway."

We'd been shuffling along in the line and my turn came, ending the conversation.

Dr. Lindbergh had started his introduction of Archie before I got back to our table— embarrassing when you're at a front table, but at least I wasn't the last one back. Myra came in later by half a minute or so.

"Dr. Dawson's book, *The Devil's Music: Murder and Mayhem in Western Folk Music*," Dr. Lindbergh was saying, "has raced to the top of the nonfiction best-seller list, while introducing the world to a field of study most people have never heard of: ethnomusicology. This branch of anthropology will, I believe, rapidly become a popular field of study as music-loving young people discover a way to use their excitement for music in a career that doesn't require vocal or instrumental performance. And so, it is my pleasure to introduce to you, although I'm certain most of you know him from past Midwest Anthropological Studies Society conferences, our keynote speaker, Dr. Archibald Finlay Dawson."

Archie bounded onto the stage, shook Charles's hand as he moved the man off the platform, then firmly planted himself behind the podium. During the applause, Myra leaned behind Naomi, motioning me to lean close.

"Dr. He's-so-bald Dawson. The ethnomusicologist everyone loves to hate."

We shared a chuckle before shifting back into our places. Archie isn't all that bald. Receding and thinning, but not bald—still, it was a cute play on his name.

"Hi everyone!" Archie's smile glinted as he acknowledged the applause of his colleagues. Then, his expression became serious and the room grew quiet, then it echoed with his words though it seemed he spoke only to me. Darkly he intoned the words of a poem. The words were familiar and Archie's spell broke as I, and a few others in the audience around me, started to chuckle while he finished reciting the first verse and chorus to "Maxwell's Silver Hammer."

Archie paused for effect. "Even the Beatles couldn't resist doing a murder song."

He got his laugh and joined right in.

"The murder song genre has been with us as long as songs have been with us. Whether commemorating an actual murder or, as in the case of Maxwell and his silver hammer, a fictional one, these songs are a way for humans to deal with the uncomfortable subject of one person taking the life of another."

Archibald went enthusiastically on and I went back to folding paper. Eventually, I ran out and needed to snitch the pad in front of Archie's empty spot at the table. I was creating a nice collection of paper figures. I really can pay better attention to a speaker when I've something to do with my hands, although I was distracted for a while as I tried to remember the name of the lady who is *the* authority on good manners. Emily Post! Perhaps she was the one responsible for the "no doing handwork while listening to a speaker" rule?

"And so," Archie concluded. I made the last fold on another crane then looked up at him. "Whether it is 'The Twa Sisters,' or as it first appears on a broadside in 1656, 'The Miller and the King's Daughter,' a song about one sister drowning another, or a modern song like '6 Feet Deep' by the rap group Gravediggaz, dealing with modern urban murder, murder songs will continue to be an important element in musical expression."

Dr. Charles Lindbergh stepped up as the applause started, shook hands with Archie, and clapped him on the back. I took advantage of everyone standing to head to the restroom again. Our music was next on the schedule; I needed to get in and out quickly since I wanted to warm up a bit before going on.

"Dr. Archibald Finlay Dawson, ladies and gentlemen," Dr. Lindbergh was saying as I wove through the applauding crowd. "There will be a break of about fifteen minutes or so and then our evening's entertainment will begin. We hope you will all stick around to hear Dr. Dawson and his friends, Dr. Jebbin Crawford, a Twombly College chemistry professor, and his wife Emory, play bluegrass music. I've been told that many of the traditional murder songs Archibald mentioned in his talk will be included, so you don't want to miss it. They will perform for half an hour, take a small break, then do another half hour, which should see our evening here ending at around eleven to eleven-thirty. See you all back here in fifteen minutes."

I beat the herd to the restroom. While in the stall, I heard a familiar voice.

"Sonya Dawson!" Myra was overly enthusiastic. "I've not seen you at one of our conferences in years. It's so good to see you."

I heard the sound of air kisses.

"Good to see you too, Myra. I just felt that I should come this year. Last minute decision. With Archie's book and all, it just seemed like I'd be missing out on all the excitement."

"Last minute, eh. I guess that explains why he said you were home sick. Does he know you're here?"

"No. I thought I'd corner . . . ah, surprise him, after he's done with his music. I didn't arrange for a room, deciding last minute as I said, so I'll be rooming with Archie. He'll need to take me there when the evening's over since I don't know where it is."

"Well, I'll see you later then, Sonya. We have all week to catch up."

"Yes, later, Myra."

They went into their stalls; I came out of mine, washed my hands, and hurried off to the small room where we'd put our instruments before the dinner started.

The first half of our gig was fun. The bluegrass favorite, "Banks of the Ohio," a traditional song, "Polly Vaughn," and the 1959 Lefty Frizzell hit "Long Black Veil" were the first set's murder songs. We also did a couple of waltzes and hot fiddle tunes so Archie could show off for his peers. Jebbin dazzled them with The Dillard's "Doug's Tune" on the banjo, and I sang a bluegrass standard, "Hot Corn, Cold Corn."

I headed for the ladies room—again—at the break and then stepped out for a breath of air. I had to walk a ways to get clear of the smokers, ending up near one corner of the Hall. I stopped short of rounding the corner when I heard voices.

"Who're you screwing over this time?"

"Screwing over?" This voice was Archie's.

"Yes. Screwing over. Using. You think I'm buying all this tripe?" I recognized Dr. Law's voice, but it was strained and raw.

Archie laughed. "Using? Really, Timmy! I think you've had a few too many drinks."

Timmy? Somehow I couldn't picture Dr. Law taking kindly to being called "Timmy."

"Oh no. No. Not too many drinks. I just know my old college roomie."

Timothy spat the words out as if they tasted foul.

"Know what about me, Timmy?"

"Just . . . just . . . Quit calling me Timmy! Whose neck do you have in the noose this time? Huh, Archie? I know you. Who are you strangling the life out of this time?"

I heard Archie's condescending chuckle and the sound of him slapping Timothy on the back. "Timmy, Timmy. You've let the murder songs get into your head! Nooses and strangling? No one's being hung or strangled, or shot or stabbed for that matter."

The tension in the air between them crept around the corner as the silence stretched on and neither man spoke. Something in my mind said I should go. I turned and tiptoed back toward the door as fast as I could. I was on the fringe of the smokers when I heard Archie's voice again, getting louder as he came around the corner.

"Maybe you ought to head back to your room for the night, Timmy old man. I really think you've had enough, both of drink and of murder songs."

"Yeah. Murder songs, or something else evil," I heard Timothy Law hiss just before I edged past the smokers and into Blythe Hall. I'd mention it to Jebbin later. For now, we had the last set to do.

The last set went well. I didn't see Dr. Law in the crowd and figured he'd left as Archie had suggested. The murder songs were "Pretty Polly," "The Lawson Murder," "Policeman," "Rose Conley," and "Poor Ellen Smith"; all traditional songs but two. "The Lawson Murder" was written about a man who murdered his family in North Carolina on Christmas Day in 1929, and "Poor Ellen Smith" is about a murder case in Winston-Salem, North Carolina in 1894. I guess they like remembering murders in song over in North Carolina. We finished with "Sow 'Em On The Mountain," a song about folks reaping what they sow. Rather an apt ending for a night featuring murder songs.

We took our bows and exited the small stage. Archie turned around as soon as we were off the platform.

"I hate to dash off; I know everyone wants to talk to me."

Talk to me, I noticed he said, not us. Typical Archibald Finlay Dawson.

"But I have to meet someone right now. I hope you two won't mind making some sort of excuse for me. I'll catch you both later this week and we'll have a nice jam session. 'Night."

With that, and without bothering to thank us for doing the gig with him, Archie dashed off through the door that led into the back area where we had warmed up. Jebbin and I didn't have much time to think about it one way or another as folks were waiting to talk to us and were obviously disappointed at the star ethnomusicologist's hasty departure.

As the clock on the county courthouse downtown tolled midnight, we headed out of Blythe Hall, instrument cases in hand, saying goodbye to John the custodian as he shut and locked the meeting room entrance doors behind us and the last of the anthropologists. The conferees turned north toward Oglethorpe Hall and their dorm rooms. Jebbin and I turned south toward Orion Fields. Jairus A.M. Twombly III had established the neighborhood on the southern edge of the campus in 1901with Frank Lloyd Wright-style Arts and Crafts houses built for the faculty. We live in one of those marvelous old homes.

"Let's cut through Fountain Garden rather than heading straight home." Jebbin's voice was warm and silky. "We can sit and neck while we listen to the water."

"What! And risk getting caught and causing a scandal?" I grabbed his arm and pulled him toward the large hedge-enclosed garden, laughing seductively. "Sounds like a fine idea to me, Dr. Crawford."

We teased and giggled our way across the lawn toward the northeast entrance through the hedge. Two walks set on compass diagonals cut the flowerbeds and lawns of the garden into quarters, meeting at the center where the fountain leaped and chuckled in an eight-pointed star-shaped pool.

Stars shone in a sky hazed with moonlight from a half moon. The fountain played its merry music. The smell of late spring flowers wafted on the cooling air. Soft lights in the fountain made the area cozy while keeping it from being scary-dark. But our playful mood faded as we saw the silhouette of someone sleeping on one of the backless benches near the fountain.

"Drat! I was looking forward to some romance." At forty-seven, I still sound like a sulky child when I'm disappointed.

"So was I." Jebbin didn't sound it though. He was too busy squinting at the figure on the bench. He nodded his head toward the figure. "Something's odd there."

I looked closer. The figure's arms both dangled down, hands resting on the ground. The legs were straight, hanging off either side of the bench in an uncomfortable-looking position. We edged closer until we could see, lit by the light of the fountain, the body of a man splayed lengthwise on the bench. Several pouches and odd amulets rested on his chest. On the ground, the hand nearest us was holding a fiddle with no strings.

Jebbin grabbed my shoulders, turning me toward the fountain and away from the bench.

"He's been strangled." Jebbin's body was tight, his voice tense. "It's Archie and he's been strangled."

CHAPTER 3

"No. I mean really, Jebbin. No. No. It can't be Archie. Can't be."

I started to look behind me at the bench and its occupant, but Jebbin took hold of my chin, preventing it. I looked up at him. The fountain framed him in a misty white aura that blended with the stars in the sky.

"We're nice stable people in the stable Midwest at a respected college in a stable little town." My oddly weightless right arm floated about with a fluttering hand at the end of it, waving about to encompass the whole of the town and campus. My left arm didn't seem to want to move.

"Well, not that there haven't been murders here befo— Murders!"

My hand stopped fluttering. I felt him wince as I gripped his arm and shook it.

"Oh my God! Jebbin! All the talk about murder songs and now Archie is . . . ah, has been . . . you know. No, that really isn't right, Jebbin."

"No, Emory. No, it isn't right. Let's go to the other side of the fountain, shall we?"

Somewhere in my head it registered that I was babbling; babbling and being led away, on wobbly legs, with Jebbin holding tightly to me. He walked so that I never did get another glimpse of that bench. The night felt colder than it had when we walked across the moonlit grounds to get to the garden. The scent of flowers was cloying, and the fountain spray on the breeze was icy.

"Where are you taking me? Shouldn't we do something? We should do something, Jebbin. We should ah . . . call the police. Yes! 9-1-1. Call them, the people at 9-1-1, and tell them that . . . Oh God. You're sure he's not just passed out?"

He sat me on the bench on the far side of the fountain, then squatted down in front of me. His face was in shadow as the only light was from the fountain behind him, but his voice sounded pale and shaky.

"Yes. I'm sure he isn't just passed out."

"Okay. You're sure. Then that means . . ."

I looked past my husband, but all I could see was the huge central sprays of the fountain with the spouting, smiling dolphins leaping around them. It seemed wrong for them to be so happy while my hollow insides shook.

"Then we need to call the police. I said that already, didn't I? Well, we do . . . need to call them and they'll come and . . ."

"They've been called."

Jebbin nearly fell over, quickly shifting one knee to the ground to avoid it. I know my rear cleared the bench by a couple of inches. Jairus and Amy Twombly drew abreast of us at the end of the northwest path.

"They will be here in a few minutes," Jairus continued. "No sirens. We'll keep this quiet as long as we can. It will be easier to handle that way. Less chance of gawkers. Did you get much of a look at him, Jebbin?"

Jebbin stood as Amy sat beside me on the bench, as though their movements were part of some graceful choreography.

"Enough. I didn't need to feel for a pulse. I'm no medical examiner but, with my knowledge of forensics, I could tell he'd been strangled."

"Fiddle strings." I interjected. Both men looked down at me.

"No, dear. It's not fiddlesticks. He really was strangled." Jebbin had the slightly exasperated tone of a parent speaking to a child who's spoken out of turn.

"No, not fiddlesticks. That would be the wood part of the bow." I was still babbling but working my way to making my point. "No. Fiddle *strings*." I started to stand but was woozier than I thought, so didn't bother. "Fiddle strings. I bet it was with fiddle strings. He had his fiddle . . ."

I closed my eyes and took a deep breath. I'm not used to talking about murdered people unless I'm telling someone about a mystery I'm reading. This wasn't fiction. I kept my eyes closed but finished my thought.

"His fiddle is in his hand. On the ground. It was near my feet and I didn't want to step on it. The strings weren't there. The bridge was off it too. The strings hold the bridge on. The pressure from . . . Sorry. Too much information."

Amy had an arm around my shoulders and I leaned into her. I felt winded, but something else came to mind.

"He has little pouches on his chest, and gaudy necklaces with large . . . ah, ah . . . what's the word? Amulets! Chintzy-looking, large amulets with symbols of the devil on them."

Amy shifted position and I could sense everyone staring at me. I opened my eyes and looked at Jebbin and Jairus.

"Well he does! I looked at the fiddle, then sort of followed his arm up to his shoulder and noticed the little lumpy things; those were the pouches and the rather tacky necklaces, and I was just about to look . . ."

My burst of energy burned out with a shiver as my eyes squeezed shut again.

"I turned her around before she saw any more," Jebbin filled in.

Jairus made an affirmative grunt. Jebbin said the police had arrived. Amy said she would help me home if Jebbin would give her the keys to our house.

I didn't say anything. I had finally run out of babble.

Amy and I hadn't gone very far, not much past the hedges around Fountain Garden, when she dropped her arm from around my shoulder along with her pretense of caring about me.

"Jam and his 'feelings'! We were almost home when he turned around, without a by-your-leave, and hauled me back here." She huffed as she wiggled her cashmere shawl back up onto her shoulders. "Knowing him, he probably knew that stuffed-shirt, ethno-whosy-whatsit guy was dead. You'd think he could have taken me home first. If he weren't a Twombly . . ." She didn't finish that thought. "The man never thinks of how things affect me."

I let her grouse. It's Amy's way. I kept myself distracted from her prattle, and thoughts of a strangled Archie lying in the Fountain Garden, by thinking about Jairus and the rest of the Twomblys. It didn't surprise me at all that Jairus knew something was amiss and came back by way of the roads on the far side of the campus, away from neighborhoods and the town proper. The Twomblys were known for their intuition. There were even some folks, back in the late 1820s after the first Jairus A. M. Twombly had established both the town of Twombly and the county of Golden that surrounds it, who reckoned the Twomblys were witches.. I know because the year after Jebbin was hired full-time, I read all the back newspapers and other local history items I could get my hands on.

The witch accusations all eventually fizzled out, but the Twomblys never lost their reputation for strangeness. They usually seemed to get what they wanted without becoming tyrants in the process. People just seemed to end up wanting what the Twomblys wanted. Not that they never had any problems, Amy being a case in point. She hornswoggled Jairus into marrying her, and he still seemed to have no idea what a harridan she was. Yet, there it is. No matter what impediments try to rise up against them, the Twomblys ride the crest. And I knew, just like Jairus had known to come to Fountain Garden tonight, that when all was said and done, Jairus would be all right and Amy wouldn't end up becoming the rich widow she expected to be.

I shook off that last thought. It had popped into my head, unbidden, and it could pop right on out again. No way no how could I know or not know that Jairus would outlive Amy.

We were to the edge of the campus when I let Amy's charming negative chatter back into my head, the better to get rid of my own disconcerting thoughts.

"Well, which one of these ancient, decrepit little houses is yours?"

I gritted my teeth in my effort to not smart off to her. The faculty houses are all lovely and well maintained. I pointed to the left end of the row of houses that faced the campus. "We're the second house from the corner."

"I suppose he expects me to stay with you or something. Cripes, he didn't even send a cop along with us, inconsiderate jerk! How am I gonna get back over there? With a dead guy by the fountain, does he think I want to walk back over there by myself?" Amy stopped, took a step back, and looked me up and down.

"You and your husband might have done that guy in! Isn't your husband one of the chemistry teachers?" She backed further away. "He . . . he could have mixed up some arsenic or something and poisoned that guy, and you've got it in that case of yours and could kill me with it when we get to your house."

Huh! What do you know; I still had my fiddle case in my left hand. I hadn't even noticed.

"Firstly, you don't make arsenic." I gave her a dramatic eye roll. "It's an element. Nothing mixes together to make arsenic. Secondly, Archie was strangled." I stopped to swallow. Saying "strangled" made my mouth go sour. "For goodness sake, call Jairus and tell him I said I'm fine, would rather be by myself, and could he send someone over to escort you home." I looked at her fine leather shoulder bag. "You do have a cell phone, don't you?"

"Well you're a great one, aren't you?" She planted her feet, jamming her fisted left hand into her hip as she waved her right arm at the campus behind her. "I walk you all the way over here and you're gonna leave me standing here on the edge of the stupid campus while you go on home?"

The woman deserved an Oscar. How she'd managed to keep Jairus fooled all these years was beyond me. As far as the rest of the community knew, she was a good enough wife and mother, so we kept quiet about the way she acted when none of the family was around. No sense stirring ashes into the soup.

"No, Amy. You just seemed afraid to come to the house with me. You're welcome to come in and call Jairus from inside. I certainly wouldn't expect you to stand out here."

She tossed our house keys in my general direction and had the call connected before we crossed the street. A cop ran up to us as I was unlocking the front door—and he was welcome to her. I walked in, locked the door behind me, and breathed in the comfort of home.

Sophie, our three-year-old golden retriever, bumped into my legs wanting to be petted. I set my fiddle case down to one side of the door and obliged her, but my initial feeling of relief had already dissipated. I leaned against the door as I locked the deadbolt, then walked unsteadily toward the kitchen, feeling as if I'd just awakened after a night filled with nightmares. Sophie padded along behind me. Even though she wasn't very old, she was good at knowing when to be calm. I turned on every light I passed. Much as I hated to open any door, I let Sophie out. And locked the door behind her. Leaning on the counter, I took the tea kettle off the back burner, filled it with water, put it back, and lit the burner.

My insides were cold. I couldn't decide between jasmine green tea or hot cocoa. Let's make this easy, I told myself, getting down two mugs, a packet of Swiss Miss sugar-free cocoa mix and the little packet with the tea bag in it. The kettle screeched, I let Sophie back in, and soon I was ensconced in my overstuffed chaise, cuddled under the afghan my Granny Merritt, my dad's ma, had knitted for me as a high school graduation present, with the steaming mugs on my chair-side table.

I pulled Jac off the table and wrapped my arms around him. Jeff Antonio Crawford, usually called Jac, is a Build-A-Bear bear Molly got me for my forty-fifth birthday. She named him after two of my favorite actors: Jeff Daniels and Antonio Banderas. Jebbin thinks he's adorable, too, and Jac goes with us on vacations and weekend trips to bluegrass festivals.

Right now, I needed a friendly presence; Jac and Granny's afghan met the need. Sophie settled on the floor beside the chaise.

I missed Molly. The house was too empty. She had only texted to say they'd arrived at their hotel in London, that she had jetlag, and would call or text later. I hadn't heard from her since. I hoped it was because she was having a great time . . . but I still wished she was staying in touch better.

And now there was this mess with Archie. I hugged Jac more tightly.

I wondered when Jebbin would get home. Amy would surely go and say to everyone that we might have done it. That hadn't occurred to me, but it would make sense for us to be suspects. After all, we obviously knew Archie. Were they giving Jebbin the third degree out there by the fountain? No! We couldn't have done it. Archie left us to mingle with the conferees after our last set and we had been there, with other people around us, until we were told it was time to close up the building.

So we were fine.

I sipped some tea, then I sipped some cocoa. They didn't mix as well as I'd hoped. The tea was healthier, but the cocoa was more comforting. I stuck with the cocoa.

I needed something to distract me. The books in the rack built into the lower part of the table by my chair were all mysteries. No. Not what I needed. I picked up the TV remote, waited for everything to switch on, then clicked to check the channel guide. Detective shows, true crime shows, cop shows, paranormal mystery shows. No, no, no and no. It appeared my choices were those, comedies I knew I didn't like, or pro wrestling. I was just about to give up when I spotted a channel running *Sweet Home Alabama*. I selected it, hugged Jac, and sighed. Hortense, our tuxedo cat, and Kumquat, our long-haired orange tabby, appeared out of nowhere, as cats are wont to do. Hortense lay down alongside my legs. Kumquat chose the back of the chair, where she could play with my hair if she wanted to.

The movie didn't work. My eyes were fixed on the TV, but my brain was elsewhere. Who could have done it? Sonya Dawson, Archie's wife, had certainly looked perturbed when I first saw her and later, when I overheard her talking to Myra, she'd sounded that way too. Had she been the person he'd rushed off to meet? But she told Myra she was going to wait until after our performance to surprise him. Unless she'd slipped an anonymous note to him saying to meet at the fountain, she couldn't have arranged the meeting without spoiling the surprise. And where *had* she gone? I hadn't seen her afterwards at all. Sonya said she was planning to share her husband's room. If she hadn't connected with him, where was she now?

And then, there was the confrontation I'd overheard between Archie and Timothy Law. They . . .

I startled and the cats went tearing off. Someone was fumbling with the front door. I looked down at Sophie. She calmly regarded the door, rose, stretched, and padded across the room as whoever it was used the brass knocker. That's not how she behaves when a stranger comes to the door. She sat down in front of the door and stared at it.

"Who is it?" I hollered as I got out of my chair.

"Your husband," was the muffled reply.

Sophie looked at me as if she was wondering how I could be so daft; of course it was Jebbin. I unlocked and opened the door.

"Why'd you lock the door? You knew I'd be coming home soon."

My husband is brilliant—and often obtuse to the simplest of

things. He came in, set his banjo case next to my fiddle case, shut and locked the door behind him, then bent to pat Sophie on the head.

"Hi, Sophie. You knew it was me, didn't ya, girl?"

"A friend of ours was murdered a few hundred yards from our home, I was here alone, and you wonder why I locked the door behind me?"

He looked up at me. I could see him processing that bit of information and then the light went on. "Oh! Yeah, that makes sense. I sort of shifted into scientist mode and didn't think about that."

"Of course. Scientist mode." My turn to be obtuse. He'd been thinking objectively at the crime scene, not thinking about his frightened, emotional wife. I gave his arm a squeeze. "You were working. I should have figured your mind was elsewhere. Are you hungry? Want some hot cocoa or something?"

He turned and hugged me. His mind had shifted to the non-analytical part of what had happened. "Yeah." His voice was weary, soft, and sad. "Yeah. Cocoa sounds great. And a grilled cheese sandwich."

We headed into the kitchen where he plopped into his usual chair and I headed for the stove to refill the tea kettle and start making the sandwiches. Yes, grilled cheese sandwiches. The warm, gooey comfort food sounded good to me as well, so I reckoned I'd join him. I'd have a fresh mug of cocoa, too. The one in the living room was cold now anyway.

"Are we suspects?" I broached the subject as I ducked into the fridge to get the sandwich fixins.

"Naw. Jairus and Amy hung around after the last set almost as long as we did. Well past the time when the murder had to have happened for Archie to have been the way he was when we found him just after midnight."

I pulled the George Foreman Grill from its spot below the under-the-cabinet coffee maker, put in the griddle plates, plugged it in, and turned it on. "That's a relief," I sighed. "Bless Amy's little heart, she suggested it was us while she walked me home. I figured I needn't worry much, since we were in the last group of people to leave the Hall." The kettle screeched and I shut off the burner. "Can you get the cocoa made, hon?"

"Yep." He got up to help. "No, we aren't suspects. Jairus is going to be using the 'Twombly Touch' and keeping things out of the media for as long as he can. I'm to call Nibodh Chatterjee in the morning to come do all the actual forensic work, but Jairus wants me there to observe."

I thought a moment as I put the sandwiches in the grill and closed it. "Conflict of interest?"

"Exactly." Jebbin carried the mugs of cocoa to the table and sat down in his chair with a sigh. "Jairus doesn't want me to let anything out of my sight, but if I actually do the work, some lawyer could scream *tampering* and all the evidence would be useless. Chatty is good. Very good. I've worked with him before." Jebbin paused before adding, "But you know that, we've had him and his family over to the house lots of times. Sorry, hon. My brain's getting fuzzy."

I nodded. Dr. Chatterjee runs a fully accredited, highly respected independent forensics laboratory in East St. Louis. His nickname suits him. Although he'd never divulge any case-related information to the press or outsiders, he is otherwise a gregarious and loquacious person with a happy personality.

"We'll need to analyze all sorts of bio samples from Archie once Antonia gets the body at the morgue. Meanwhile, Chatty and I can get to work right away on all those little pouches that were on his chest. The forensics guys opened one. It was full of dried herbs of some sort, and they figure that's what's in the others as well. We'll have lots of mass spectrometer and gas chromatograph work to do. Jairus wants the hospital lab and us to both run everything."

Bio samples from Archie.

I almost dropped the sandwich I was removing from the grill. I felt woozy again. Jebbin was slipping back into scientist mode and I guess I wasn't quite capable of that degree of emotional distance. Not yet, anyway. We were still talking about a man we had known for years, even if we weren't what I'd call close. A man we had shared meals and music with.

I wasn't ready to think about Archie's bio samples yet.

"So." I set the sandwiches at our places and sat down across from Jebbin. "This is going to keep everyone busy for most of the summer, I suppose. Good thing you don't have summer classes to teach."

"Ah! Woo! Ahh! Ac-choo-ally naw," Jebbin mumbled around a bite of hot cheese sandwich. It happens all the time and, considering how smart he is, you'd think he'd learn. He rarely remembers to let hot food cool. He took a few moments to finish that bite and swallow it, during which time I got him a glass of water. Hot cocoa wouldn't help his overheated tongue.

"Thanks, hon." He gulped half the glass down. "Whew! Guess I'll let that sit a bit. Where were we . . . oh yeah. Busy all summer. No. Jairus wants it solved before the anthropology society's conference is over."

"What!" Half a sandwich was on its way to my mouth to be blown on to cool it. It stopped midway. "That's a week, Jebbin. That's only one week."

"Yep, one whole week. Jairus wants it all kept out of the media as much as possible and to that end wants it, as he put it, 'cleared up by the end of the conference.' He also said it was 'best to get it taken care of while the suspects are all still here.' I think he watches too many mystery and cop shows."

"Well, I can give you a couple people to start with."

His dark eyebrows rose above the top rim of his glasses. "Oh. Really?"

"Yes really." I was instantly on the defensive. "I heard some conversations and . . ."

"That's hearsay."

"I know. But," I gave him my smug look, "saying I heard people talking about Archie and talking to Archie in ways that made it clear they had issues with the man is enough to question them, isn't it?"

"True." He took a bite of sandwich, now reasonably cool, though I could tell his mouth was still tender. "So what did you hear?"

I leaned toward him, eager to spill the beans. "Well for one thing, his wife is here, or was here last night. Myra Fordyce pointed her out to me in the ladies room, and later I heard the two of them talking in there. She, Archie's wife that is, was planning on surprising him by showing up for all the hoopla over his book. Sonya was planning on making it an even bigger surprise by sharing his dorm room with him." I had his full attention now. "I didn't see when she left. She couldn't have been around for long after the last set because I didn't see her in the crowd that stayed. She'd said she was going to present herself to him after we were all done performing and let him know then about rooming with him."

"Hmm . . . that certainly gives her a reason to meet up with him after the set and to want it to be somewhere private. She could've been planning to kil—" Jebbin must have caught the look on my face. "Ah . . . she could have had all those pouches, amulets, and stuff in her purse."

I nodded. "Then, during the break between sets, Dr. Timothy Law and Archie had an intense discussion just around the southwest corner of the Hall."

This time Jebbin's jaw dropped a bit. "And just how do you know that? You weren't tailing Archie, were you?"

"No, of course not." I took a couple of bites of my sandwich and swigged some cocoa before continuing. "I stepped out for some fresh air, only there wasn't any by the doors 'cause all the smokers were there. I walked off to get away from the smokers. I'd intended to go around the corner but stopped when I heard their voices."

"And," he raised an eyebrow and grinned knowingly, "you just had to stop and listen instead of turning around and heading back toward the door."

"Well, yes! I mean, I know . . . ah, knew Archie, and I'd met Dr. Law that morning and he'd seemed such a nice sort that I just had to find out why he sounded so vindictive."

Jebbin pulled over one of the small pads of paper and a pencil we keep on the kitchen table. He was looking down, but I could tell he was grinning.

"Okay, Sherlock. We've got Archie's wife . . ."

"Sonya."

"Right, Sonya. And we have Dr. Law."

"Dr. *Timothy* Law."

He looked up. "Anyone else?"

"Not that I know of yet, though Myra seemed to know a lot about Archie. And I'm not Sherlock Holmes."

"No?"

I'm sure I did the Cheshire Cat proud. "No. I'm a young Jane Marple."

CHAPTER 4

Jebbin and I talked until four in the morning, when we finally shuffled off to bed and to sleep—in a mostly awake sort of way. Jebbin was up and gone to the lab by six. I gave up on dozing, did some in-bed stretching, and rose at ten after seven.

I was in a funk. Jebbin got to run off and do something constructive whilst I got to stay home and . . . do what I always did. Housework. Hobbies. Take Sophie for walks. Volunteer at the library. Much as I had joked about being a young Miss Marple, I didn't much feel like her. I shuffled into the kitchen, still in my jammies. I pulled out the water container for the coffee maker with a limp-fish grip, took it to the sink, let the water dribble unenthusiastically into it, then stuck it back in place. My finger went for the machine's "on" switch when it stopped, hovering just short of making contact.

Wait a minute.

I mean, after all, what did Jane do? She approached people as a sweet, kindly, understanding old lady and they opened up to her. She'd sit and knit—and listen in on conversations. She'd see everything.

What Would Jane Marple Do?

I smiled as I got dressed.

Jebbin had mentioned that Jairus told him they were going to gather all the conferees into the auditorium at nine thirty to inform them of the murder and to start questioning them.

I let Sophie out, fed the cats, grabbed my knitting caddy and, stuffing my house keys, phone, and library keycard into it, I headed out the door. W.W.J.M.D.? I was not officially invited, but there was no way I was missing the buffet breakfast Fiorello would be serving the MASS group . . . nor the meeting afterward.

I heard Myra before she got anywhere near me.

"Emory! Didn't expect you to be here." She pulled up alongside me at the omelet station. "Did you notice the posters on all the doors? They were even posted on all the doors in the dorms. Twombly College wants us all to meet in the auditorium at nine o'clock. Some sort of something we have to know before the workshops and presentations begin, although it will be putting us off schedule because everything was supposed to start at nine."

She finally paused to breathe, caught the luscious scent of my omelet cooking, and leaned toward the table. "Do you know what's up? That omelet smells divine! I think I'll have one myself, young lady, when you're finished making hers."

The culinary student smiled and nodded. "Be choosing your fillings then, ma'am, this one's nearly done."

"No," I lied in response to Myra's question. "I've no idea at all what's going on. I came for an omelet, toast made from Fiorello's whole grain bread, and his legendary cinnamon rolls."

"Hmm . . . yes. I can smell those too." She looked along the buffet. "My God! They're huge! I have *got* to have one of those."

I grinned. My omelet smelled "divine" and her un-believed-in God was invoked over the cinnamon rolls. Perhaps the Hutterites had had more effect on her than she realized. On the other hand, it at least showed how pervasive religious terms have become in our language.

I waited with her while the cook prepared her omelet, and then we attacked the rest of the buffet. Each balancing two heaping plates—which did include (between the two of us) some orange wedges, fresh peach and pineapple slices, strawberries, and cantaloupe in amongst the omelets, bacon, sausages, biscuits and gravy, toast, and cinnamon rolls—we headed for two spots at a nearby table where earlier I'd stashed my knitting caddy. The servers brought coffee. Myra had Earl Grey tea and we both had cranberry juice.

We didn't talk much as we ate. It's just plain wrong to interrupt the savoring of a masterpiece. But eventually our rapt consumption slowed.

"You know . . ." Myra craned her neck to look around the room. "I don't see the poster boy for ethnomusicology. Have you seen dear Archie?"

It's amazing how well a nice person like myself can lie. How smoothly one can cover one's emotions. How, if you work hard at it, you can manage to neither spit out nor choke on the food in your mouth when startled. I paused. Deep breath in through the nose. Good. Good. A slow sip of coffee to gracefully wash it all down. And answer.

"No, I haven't. Maybe he plans to miss the . . . ah, the, um . . . important thingy that they need y'all to know this morning. Maybe he already knows about it." Oh, yes. In some way, on some level of existence, I was sure Archibald Finlay Dawson knew he was dead.

Myra kept looking around. "She's not here either. You know, Naomi. Can't see her anywhere."

"Well, she is his teaching assistant. She probably already knows, too." My turn to beseech God to intervene. I reckoned they had pulled Naomi aside and told her the news separately. She would have noticed right away that her mentor wasn't around and would have started asking others if they'd seen him, quite nicely ruining the effect I'm sure Jairus was hoping for with his announcement. Please,

Lord, help Jairus not drag his big reveal out too long. I wouldn't know for a while if the Lord would inspire Jairus Twombly, but He'd helped me out of this tight situation.

"What workshops are you taking today, Myra?"

I sighed with relief as she dove into descriptions of her day's agenda, and that kept her busy until Dr. Lindbergh went to the microphone. He got everyone's attention, then announced it was a quarter to nine. Time to wind up our meal and head to the auditorium.

By a quarter after nine, the first several rows of the auditorium were full and Jairus stood center stage at a podium.

Jairus did a long, slow scan of the room. As his gaze passed over them, I could see people leaning toward him like iron filings toward a magnet. The Twombly Touch.

"Good morning, everyone. I do apologize for this interruption of your agenda. I hope the excellence of Fiorello's cooking has made it a bearable experience."

The pleasantry didn't loosen his pull on us. We all leaned in further.

"I have taken upon myself the duty of informing you of a tragic incident that occurred on this campus last night after the end of your evening program. One of your fellow conferees, Dr. Archibald Finlay Dawson, was found dead in Fountain Garden. And, before you ask . . ." Jairus paused to look over his audience, ". . . he was murdered."

The crowd's reaction was delayed by the immensity of what he said. I felt their stunned silence, then heard gasps and whispers.

"Due to that," Jairus continued as the crowd hushed, "there are certain considerations, requests, and restrictions that we have to place on you all. We are asking that you refrain from contacting the media. We are asking that you do not call friends, relatives, or colleagues who are not here to tell them about this heinous event."

The conferees sat staring at the man at the podium, soaking in his words as though mesmerized. If I hadn't known what was coming, I would have been enthralled too. Even so, I could feel his charisma.

"I know, in this day of instant everything, of cell phones, and smart phones, and computers, it seems a ludicrous request. But, it is the intention of this institution, of the Twombly Police Department and the Golden County Sheriff's Department, to solve this crime within the week of this conference. This will be impossible if we have to take precious time to deal with the media. No information will be withheld once the murderer is brought into custody, but we would like the freedom to work as quickly as possible."

People around me were nodding as though this all made perfect sense to them as two men I recognized stepped onto the platform.

"All of you will be interviewed individually by Lieutenant Jason Anderson of the Twombly City Police." Jairus gestured to the man on his right. "And by Captain Henry Schneider of the Golden County Sheriff's Department." Jairus gestured to his left. Jason and Henry nodded as they were mentioned.

"At this early stage, we don't consider anyone in particular to be a suspect," Jairus went on. "Sorry to say, at this point every conferee is a suspect. We ask that you go on with your conference. I spoke with Dr. Lindbergh and arrangements have been made in case a presenter is unable to give their lecture. These substitutes will be filling Dr. Dawson's slots. We thank you for your cooperation."

Jairus took a last slow look at the crowd, nodded to them, then left the stage. As the crowd came out of their daze, most of them rose from their seats to mill around in the aisles and spilled out into the lobby, jabbering in a rush of emotion. I had grabbed my caddy as he was winding up and I wandered like a ghost amongst them, watching and listening.

Timothy Law looked hungover because he was. Mind you, his clothes looked tidy, face scrubbed and shaved, hair all neatly combed. But his complexion was sallow and puffy around his eyes. He was talking with a man I didn't know.

"Can they do that?" his companion bellowed.

Timothy winced. "Keep the volume down, Fred. Yes, they can do that. Actually, if they decide someone's suspicious, they can most likely keep them here longer than the week of the conference."

"Why would they just suspect one of us? There's a whole bunch of people on campus and a whole town just a block or two away."

"It's the way these things go, I think. The first suspects are usually family members, then close friends, then they carry it on from there." Timothy rubbed his forehead and sighed. "A lot of us at the conference knew Archie to one degree or another, so we're the first group they need to go through. I mean, he's married, but his wife isn't with him. So that leaves us."

I spotted Henry Schneider of the Sheriff's Department's homicide division and Detective Jason Anderson of the Twombly city police walking up to the two men. Henry looked down at his notebook.

"Excuse me."

Timothy jumped, then turned to face the Captain as he and Fred both said, "Yes" in unison.

"Which one of you is Dr. Timothy Law?"

Timothy's right hand slid up level with his shoulder. "I'm Dr. Law."

"If you'll come with us, sir?"

He nodded. "Catch ya later, Fred," he said in parting, voice resigned and shoulders slumping. He turned to follow the officers as I slipped away in another direction. After a few steps I paused, took my phone out of my knitting caddy, went to the notepad, and jotted a couple of quick notes:

Dr. Law one of first interviewed. (they must have got the information I gave to Jebbin last night)

Remember to invite Jason over for supper tonight. See if he'll talk about today's interviews while I ply him with my lasagna.

It's a perk, all the stuff you can do on a phone. Whereas people would notice someone jotting notes in a notebook, no one thinks twice about someone messing around with their phone. My note taking wouldn't attract any unwanted attention.

Dr. Lindbergh's voice came over the speakers as he announced that the first lectures and workshops would begin in fifteen minutes. I carefully closed in on Cameron, noting on my phone that I needed to find out her full name.

"It *is* a shock." She was leaning in to speak to a heavy-set man. "Not that I knew Dr. Dawson well, mind you. He never missed a conference and neither did I, so I did get to know him somewhat, but conferences were the extent of our contact."

"I didn't know him well, either." The man shook his head. "You know, surface impressions, that sort of thing. He always seemed rather full of himself, which I find terribly off-putting, so I never bothered to get to know him any better. However, it didn't surprise me that he'd have a book that would be such a hit. He knew how to sell himself, I'll give him that much."

"Hmm, yes. Sell himself." She tucked her hair behind her right ear. "Yes, Dr. Dawson knew how to do that."

"Well, Dr. Garrow, I'm presenting one of the first workshops, so I'd best be off. I'm all set up in my room, but it's always best to be there early when you're the presenter." The portly anthropologist winked, chuckled, and held out his hand while I noted *Dr. Cameron Garrow* on my phone.

"Of course, Dr. Simmons." Dr. Garrow shook his hand. "I'm signed up for Dr. Martin's lecture on Pre-Revolutionary War Idioms. It's part of my field of study, but you never know when you might pick up something you've not heard before. Perhaps we'll catch up with each other later."

With parting nods, they left, going in opposite directions. I started to leave as well. The crowd was thinning, and my standing about eavesdropping would be noticeable. But on my way I had an inspiration. If I was going to talk to people to learn all I could, the perfect one to start with was Myra. I caught up with her and asked her to join me for lunch at the Sit & Sup Cafe a few blocks off campus. We arranged to meet at the foot of the Hall's main staircase at twelve forty-five, since the conference was now that far off schedule, then went our separate ways.

I jogged up the stairs to the library.

"Mrs. Crawford, guess what!" Cindy, a student worker, greeted me with wide, frightened-looking eyes. "There's been a murder on campus!"

"I know. How did you know?"

"My boyfriend works on the kitchen and banquet staff and he also runs the sound and lights in the auditorium. When he came in to work breakfast, Fiorello told him he was to leave at nine forty-five to work the lights and sound for Mr. Twombly. Jerry said Mr. Twombly himself announced it to the people at that conference that's going on this week. Said it was some Dr. Somebody or Other who was part of the conference. Can you imagine?"

"Barely, Cindy." It still gave me chills. I waved my hand toward the anthropology display, which included several copies of Archie's book. "It was the man who wrote that book."

"Whoa!" She shivered and gasped. "I wonder if he'll haunt the library now." She trembled again, then looked at me, more excited now than scared. "The cops brought some people up here and said they'd be using the conference rooms most of the day. Guess they're gonna question them like they do on TV."

"Yes . . . I would reckon so."

I looked over to the row of three conference rooms. They are part of the original library, not the areas of the building that have, over the years, been remodeled into library space. Each room has large windows in the wall and a door facing into the library, but the windows also have shutters that can be closed to give privacy. When college groups used the rooms, the rules were that the window in the door had to remain uncovered, but this didn't apply to the police, apparently, as every window was shuttered. An idea formed in my head. There was a small, staff-only workroom between the first and second conference rooms, isolating that one room from the others. Usually, people nabbed that room first since they figured it would give more privacy, and they'd be right for the general public. But I knew that it was possible to hear quite a bit of what was being said in the rooms on either side from inside the workroom. Ah, yes... W.W.J.M.D.?

"Well, Cindy, I'm going to go work on the paranormal section some more. I started on it yesterday but kept getting pulled away for other things."

"OK, Mrs. Crawford. Maybe you'll get some hints about that murdered guy possibly haunting the library." She smiled. "You know, wanting to see if anyone checks out his book."

I laughed along with her and then headed off, going past the display. It wouldn't surprise me at all if Archie did just that. I went to the paranormal section and past it, circling around to the workroom and letting myself in with a swipe of my keycard. Voices came from both rooms. Conference room two had a female voice in it; one was all males. I figured, since Dr. Law was probably a main suspect, they had him in the more isolated room, so I moved to that wall.

The vents are hard to spot, down by the floor where they blend in with the baseboard. They didn't line up from room to room, but you could still hear better down by the vent than you could just standing in the workroom. I resigned myself to being stiff and achy as the price for the better acoustics and lay down on the cold, hard, vinyl floor. They had finished the general information part of the questioning and had gotten to more pertinent matters.

"Yes, I had an argument with Archie, Dr. Dawson, last night. How did you know?"

I could picture thin, scholarly looking, hungover Timothy Law sitting at the old oak library table. It was probably as uncomfortable as any interrogation room at either the police station or the sheriff's office as there are no pads on the oak, Mission-style chairs.

"You weren't exactly someplace private, Dr. Law." That was Lieutenant Jason Anderson. Timothy was in with the big guns. There was a slight pause as, I'm sure, Jason checked his notes. "You were outside Blythe Hall at the southwest corner of the building."

"Yeah, yeah. It's just that, well, we had walked away from all the smokers and were around the corner out of sight. We thought we were somewhat alone."

No one spoke. I pictured him looking up at Jason and Captain Henry Schnider, realizing they weren't going to say anything.

"Ah, yes. Um. So we had an argument. It was all ancient history. Well, not like what you might think is ancient to anthropologists, but our own ancient history. Archie's and mine. We were roommates in undergrad and grad school. Well, through getting our masters. By the time we were done with that, we were past the roommate stage. But in our senior year of college he stole my girlfriend. We had some other academic quibbles, but that was it."

There was another pause, broken by Henry.

"So, what got you two rehashing ancient history?"

"Archie was bragging about being there with this year's teaching assistant. She's a real knockout, in case you don't know who she is by now. Naomi something. It sounds sort of Russian. At any rate, he was bragging that he could still get the hot girls while I was still single and at the conference by myself. I was drunk enough that it just got it all going, if you get what I'm saying. Between him getting all the attention over his book and razzing me about women, I just lost it and blew up at him."

"What happened after the argument?"

"Ah, we . . . ah, that's Archie and I, we walked back toward the doors into the building where all the smokers were finishing up. He was telling me I should go back to my room, skip the rest of his bluegrass gig, and sleep it off. I was thoroughly sick and tired of him by that point and decided that was a good idea. I wouldn't have to hear him or look at him or watch everyone fawn over him after he was done performing. So, yeah, I went back to my room in the dorm and went to bed."

"And that's it?" Jason asked.

"Yes, sir. That's it. I slept like the dea . . . like a log, till my alarm went off."

I eased up off the floor. Just in case Cindy or some other library staffer came looking for me in the paranormal stacks, I reckoned I'd best get out of the workroom. I was stiff and sore, but it was worth it. What Timothy had just told the police and what I had overheard between him and Archie last night outside of the Hall didn't seem to dovetail. All the attendees knew ahead of time that Archie was the main speaker for the conference. Timothy would have had lots of time to plan everything, right down to pulling Archie aside to have an argument that could easily end with a challenge to meet him later in the garden.

CHAPTER 5

I kept an eye on the time while I worked on the paranormal section and got to the bottom of the main staircase just as Myra arrived from her last workshop/lecture before lunch. We walked the four blocks to the Sip & Sup and were soon all set for a food and gossip session.

Myra shook her napkin out to cover her navy-blue polyester pants. Her yellow cotton blouse with tiny dark blue flowers on it was partially hidden by a navy-blue sweater. The walk over had brought a blush to her round cheeks. She took a few moments to look around the room.

"This reminds me of the café in the town near my Hutterite friends up in North Dakota. Hope the food's as good."

I laughed. "They all look basically the same, you know, these small-town cafes. And yes, the food is delightful. They make a lot of it from scratch."

We perused the menu. I had a chicken salad sandwich platter and Myra had the Reuben platter. Diet colas completed our orders and Sally, the owner's grown daughter, ran off to give the order to John or Mary Ellen, her dad and mom, who did all the cooking. What can I say; I've lived here over thirty years. You get to know most of the residents after that many years in a small town.

I delivered my opening remark. "So, Myra. What do you think of all this? The murder and all, I mean."

"Whew!" She fanned herself with her hand. "A hot time at the MASS conference this year. I bet it'll be the only time people will actually care about reading the minutes from a conference. I'll have to do an extra special good job on them."

She laughed heartily, then sipped some of her soda before continuing.

"But seriously. I never would have thought it. Not at our conference with our little bunch. Mind you, this is the largest attendance we've had in . . . well, ever. And it's all 'cause of Archie's book. So there's a bunch of folks I don't know as well. That said," Myra leaned closer to me, "if it was going to happen, it doesn't surprise me one tiny bit that dear Dr. 'He's-So-Bald' Finlay Dawson would be the victim. The man could charm the rattle off a snake, but he could also feel like a pebble in your shoe. I never really trusted his unctuous bonhomie."

She took another sip of soda while getting out of Sally's way as she set down our plates. We ate a few bites without comment, Myra making yummy noises and nodding while I grinned as well as I could around my bites of savory chicken salad on a whole grain bun that I knew had been baked this morning. I never had chicken salad anywhere else. No one else's compared to Mary Ellen's.

"This food is as good as the café in North Dakota." Myra declared when she finally paused in her enthusiastic eating. "For some reason, they just don't understand how to make a proper Reuben. I couldn't resist giving it a try here and it's to die for. Thanks for inviting me. Back to what I was saying, I suppose it's much more interesting to try to figure out which one of us charming know-it-alls did the deed. While I could easily see Archibald being a murder victim, I have more of a problem seeing the rest of us as potential killers."

Myra gave me a piercing look that stopped my sandwich midway to my mouth.

"What do you know about it?" she challenged me. "I mean, after all, your husband teaches forensic science as well as chemistry. I looked him up in one of the college catalogs on the information table after you left."

OK. To be honest, I hadn't planned on anyone asking *me* questions, only me asking *them* questions. Hadn't planned on it, so hadn't thought about it, so hadn't come up with good answers ready to hand. I could hear the whirring of gears in my mind. I took a big, slow bite of my sandwich to give myself some time to think. I knew quite a bit, obviously. And, yes, he was in on the investigation. But (oh such a huge but) how much should I say? I gestured toward my mouth while holding up my index finger. Myra nodded and took a bite of her own sandwich while waiting for me to chew and swallow.

"Well, ah, yeah. I know a little about it, but not much. Jebbin's been asked to help with the investigation, but only in a limited way. Seeing as the murder occurred on the campus and Jebbin works for the college, it was decided that some lawyer could scream conflict of interest if he did any of the actual analysis. He's merely observing while an outside forensic scientist does the work."

There. This was beginning to remind me of the fencing class I took at Twombly. Thrust and parry. I felt pretty good with that answer. But Myra recovered with a solid riposte.

"Even if he's only helping, he surely knows some of the details."

"Ye-e-s-s. I'm sure he does by now. But I've not seen or talked to him since he was called into the lab early this morning. So . . ." I raised both hands palms up in the traditional "I know nothing" sign. I was being truthful, which is the best sort of lie. I hadn't talked to Jebbin since he left for the lab. Myra sighed and nodded. I went on the offensive.

"But you know a lot of the conferees. Any you know of who had possible problems with Archie? Oh!" A bolt of insight hit me. "What about his wife? You pointed her out to me in the ladies last night. Said she hadn't been to a conference in ages. What about, ah . . . whats-her-name?"

Lunge, touché, and point to me. The challenge faded from Myra's eyes as she frowned.

"Sonya."

Myra took another bite of her Reuben, shoved some chips in after it, and chewed while I watched the thoughts go by in her eyes.

"Yes, Sonya is a definite possibility I suppose. She's Greek and feisty. Her father wasn't poor when he came to the states, and he's quite wealthy now. It's easy to see why she and Archie were attracted to each other; they met in college I think. You know, both were gorgeous to look at and both loved the things money can buy. Only, I don't think it owns her like it does . . . um, did, Archie. I think she worked in her dad's restaurants as a kid."

Myra finished half her sandwich then flagged Sally down and asked for a box for the rest. She returned to our conversation with a sigh.

"But I'm pretty sure he's hurt her. There's hurt in her eyes, and I know Archie is far from loyal, if you catch my drift. Since about ten or fifteen years ago, he stopped showing up to the conferences with Sonya and started showing up with teaching assistants. Always cute, always stacked, always female TAs."

"Like Naomi." I rolled my eyes. "Although I'll admit, after talking to her last night, she's actually a rather nice, intelligent girl."

"Yes. And I don't think he's had his way with her yet. She seemed uncomfortable with the way he put his arm around her at the registration table yesterday."

I nodded. I had been right about Myra. She was nosy and she noticed details. She was going to be a great source of information.

We were running out of lunchtime.

"What about Dr. Law? When he left the registration table yesterday, I could hear him talking to someone in a grumpy sort of way, and then Archie and Naomi came around the corner."

"Hmm. Could be something there, yes. Rumor has it, and it's a long-standing rumor, that little Timothy liked to steal other people's writing back in college and that Archie, being his roommate, knew about it."

"Could Archie have been holding that over his head or something?"

"Wouldn't surprise me. Dear Archibald certainly had something on Timothy. It was fairly easy to see Timothy would rather not be around Archie, yet Archie seemed to make of point of keeping Timothy close by. He'd always sit near him at meals and such at every conference, and he never missed an opportunity to razz or embarrass Timothy."

"That does sound unpleasant for Dr. Law."

As if on cue, Timothy Law walked into the café. Myra and I were not in his direct line of vision from the entrance, so he didn't see us as Sally greeted him and showed him to a booth. Myra checked her watch.

"Well, m'dear, I'm teaching a workshop at two thirty and it's nearly two. I'd best be heading back to the school to get ready."

"Oh!" I started to flag Sally down for the check while looking at my mostly uneaten lunch sitting on my plate.

"No, no, no, Emory. No, you sit and enjoy your lunch. I see the cash register over there, I'll just go pay my part of the tab and be on my way." She patted my shoulder. "So nice of you to ask me to have lunch with you. I usually just eat on the campus of whatever college the conference is at. It was nice seeing more of the town. Maybe we can do it again during the week and you can share any tidbits you get from your hubby."

That again. I'm not wanting to share information *with* her, I want to get it *from* her, but I was thinking I might have to do a little of the latter to keep getting the former.

"Sure, Myra. Jebbin usually does tell me some things, though he has to be careful. Ethics issues, you know."

"Of course. I should have thought of that. Well, you can tell me what he can tell you." She laughed lightly, patting my shoulder again. "See you later, Emory."

I watched her go. She didn't glance toward the booth Timothy was in, and I couldn't see him, but if he did spot her, he didn't speak to her as she paid and left without looking his way. She did, however, nearly run over Sonya Dawson as she came in. They exchanged a few words, most likely Myra offering her condolences, and then parted. Sonya went straight for the booth where Timothy Law was sitting. I asked Sally for a box for my sandwich and chips and thought about Friday night while she went to fetch it.

I assumed Sonya was there for part of the performance, but I wasn't really sure. The last I saw her, or heard her to be more precise, was in the ladies room talking to Myra before the first set. But I thought I'd seen her sitting at an empty table outside the light from the stage where it was hard to tell who anyone was. That table was totally empty during the second set. Timothy I knew was at the first set but not the second.

Sally brought the Styrofoam box. I packed up my leftovers, went to the register, paid, and left. I did take a look at the two of them from outside. Sonya might have noticed me, but she hadn't been introduced to me nor had I met her after our performance, so I doubt she recognized me. I watched them for a moment, talking with their heads close over the table, before I walked away. How interesting that they were both unaccounted for from the second set on, exactly when Archie's murder was being set up.

CHAPTER 6

I was busy shelving returned books, an endless task at most libraries. The Twombly College library had grown quite large because it also served as the town's public library. We're open every day of the week with shorter hours on Sundays. Even when school isn't in session, we're still busy.

"Emory."

I jumped, gasped, and dropped the book I was about to shelve. With my hand over my heart and panting for breath, I looked up into the warm, brown face of Detective Lieutenant Anderson, who was grinning from ear to ear.

"Glad you think it's funny. You just shortened my life. Scoundrel."

"Naw. Added to it from what I've read lately. Fitness folks all say it gets your heart going like good exercise does."

"You're like a naughty little brother."

He grinned wider, then put on a businesslike expression. "If you'll come with me, ma'am, I'm taking you in for questioning in regards to the murder of Dr. Archibald Finlay Dawson. We want the facts, ma'am. Just the facts. And you better not make me write out that guy's full name too many times." He gave me an exaggerated wink. "Always wanted to talk to someone like that. All old TV-cop-show style. But really, we need to get your version of last night since you and Jebbin found him. I was serious about the name thing though. Lord have mercy! What a pain to write out all the time. He musta hated book signings."

Jebbin worked with the Twombly police often, and with Jason in particular. He and his family had been to our house many times since he'd been made a detective. I wrapped my arm around one of his muscular ones.

"You may escort me to your interrogation room, Detective Anderson. I will do my best to stick to 'the facts, ma'am, just the facts.'"

We sauntered off toward the conference room Timothy Law had been in this morning.

"Sit down, please, Mrs. Crawford." Captain Henry Schneider waved me to one of the oak mission chairs at the old library table while Jason shut the door behind us. It was no surprise that Henry was more formal. He and Jebbin had clashed the first time they met, and things had never improved. Whether it was Jebbin's southern Missouri accent and country boy manners or his good relationship with Jairus Twombly or whatever, we never could figure out what the problem was. Unfortunately, it often got in the way of Jebbin's forensic work for the sheriff's department. I would have rather talked to Jason, but you can't always have what you want.

Henry looked at his notes. "Do you mind if we record this interview, Mrs. Crawford?"

"Not at all, Captain Schneider."

He jotted my response in his notes, then turned on a small recorder.

"This interview is being recorded on Saturday, June 7, 2011, with the consent of the interviewee, with Detective Lieutenant Jason Anderson of the Twombly City Police Department and Captain Henry Schneider of the Golden County Sheriff's Department present. Please state your full name."

"Emory Mary Crawford. I'm the wife of Dr. Jebbin Crawford,

professor of chemistry and forensic science at Twombly College. I'm a homemaker and I volunteer at the college library."

All right, it was more than he asked for, but I figured he was going to ask it anyway and thought I'd save some time. Fortunately, Henry didn't seem too ruffled by it.

"Ah, thank you, Mrs. Crawford. What were you doing at the dinner for the Midwest Anthropologic Studies Society last night? That being Friday, June 6, 2011?"

"Well, Jebbin and I might not have been at the dinner, since we aren't part of that group, but we had been included as after-dinner entertainers. But we are, eh, were friends of their featured speaker for the conference, Dr. Archibald Finlay Dawson."

I glanced at Jason. He glanced heavenward, then grinned at me.

"He invited us to sit at his table for dinner as well. Oh. He was also part of the performance with Jebbin and me."

"You and Dr. Crawford sat with Dr. Dawson?"

"Yes."

"Did you notice anything unusual about him that evening? Or anything about anyone else at the table?"

"No."

"Did you know anyone else at the table ahead of time?"

"Yes, I met Ms. Myra Fordyce and Ms. Naomi Malkoff that morning. I worked a shift at the Twombly College welcome table next to the registration table for the conference. Ms. Fordyce was their registrar and Ms. Malkoff was with Dr. Dawson when they registered."

I paused and relaxed a little. "Well, technically, I didn't meet Naomi at that time. I saw her with Archie and heard him introduce her to Myra, so I knew who she was before I was introduced to her at the dinner."

"Hmm."

Henry was being monosyllabic. I looked at Jason and shrugged.

"Henry?" I was surprised when he piped up.

The captain turned an annoyed eye to the police detective. "Hmm?"

"It might save some time and be more informative to just let her tell us what she remembers from last night."

Henry closed his eyes and drew a deep breath, obviously holding back a flash of temper. "Yeah, yeah." He looked at me as if daring me to step out of line in any way. "So, Mrs. Crawford, what do you remember about last night's events? Don't be shy. We aren't going to hurt you or bully you. You just tell us in your own way whatever it is you recall."

Lord love us all, the sarcasm was puddling on the table top and dribbling over the edge onto the floor.

"Of course, Captain Schneider." I proceeded to tell him every little detail in an organized and concise fashion. Yes, I can be organized and concise when I really have to be. I finished up with Jebbin and I discussing Jairus's order about solving the case in six days and what we thought about it before we headed off to bed.

"And I don't think you need to know what happened in our bed, Captain, so I'm done."

"Hmm."

Then we sat there in silence while the battery clock on the wall ticked. And ticked. Henry looked through his file. Tapped his pencil to the off beat of the clock.

"Guess that covers most everything, Mrs. Crawford."

He looked up so quickly I startled.

"Let me warn you, Mrs. Crawford. We know your husband is observing all the lab work. We figure he'll talk to you, as much as you'll understand, about some of it. We also know you volunteer here at the library and will be around the campus."

He leaned in toward me. I instinctively leaned away.

"Stay out of police business, Mrs. Crawford. Do I make myself clear?"

My hands were in my lap and I hastily crossed my fingers.

"Of course, Captain. As you say, I'm not as knowledgeable as you or my husband. Heavens, I barely have a bachelor's degree! Mind you, I can't be unsociable either. If I'm engaged in conversation by any of the conferees, including the ones I've come to know somewhat, I can't very well not talk to them. That would make the college look bad."

To my great satisfaction, I could see him raring up to light into me. I cut him off before he could. "But, Captain Schneider, I will do my best to be as unforthcoming as I possibly can." I grinned, showing most of my teeth. "Will that suffice?"

Henry flopped back in his uncomfortable oak chair, waving his hand at the door as he did. "Yeah, yeah. You can leave. I'm . . . we're done with you for now."

Jason rose, opened the door for me, and followed me out. I raised an eyebrow at him. "Do I need an escort? Need to make sure I don't talk to anyone?"

"What? No!" He relaxed and giggled, which always sounded weird coming from the hefty former wrestler. "Naw. I've got to toddle off to pull in the next person on the list for questioning. Which is actually your husband. Mr. Twombly didn't want him pulled out of the lab, but Henry insisted that, since he found the body, he needed to be officially questioned."

I put my hand on Jason's arm to stop him.

"If I won't get into too much trouble for talking to you—wink, wink, nudge, nudge— I'll take this opportunity to invite you over for supper tonight. Lasagna."

His eyes widened along with his grin. Oh yeah. I had him hooked.

"Just work out a time with Jebbin and Chatty, he's invited too. Have Jebbin text the time to me, and I'll see you all tonight."

"I'll let Diane know as well. She won't mind. Most likely wasn't expectin' me home for dinner anyway with the murder case just gettin' on. I need to get moving, Emory. See you later!"

As he walked away, he pumped his fist and murmured, "Yes! Lasagna!"

I grabbed a few books from the folklore section, stopped by the checkout desk to check them out, stopped by the main desk to sign myself out for the day, and then headed home. I had some research to do and lasagna to make.

My house smelled wonderful. The lasagna was perfection and the men folk were more than willing to talk about their day's work. Chatty is Hindu, but not a very strict one. Mostly to increase the general comfort level of the meal, I made the lasagna with turkey sausage and lamb instead of my usual beef and pork sausage. He was on his second helping, and I was wondering if he might lick his plate clean, he was so enraptured.

He smacked his lips. "This is miraculous, Emory." He drank a sip of his tea before continuing with the conversation. "I will admit I was surprised when I read in Antonia's notes that there were five instrument strings. My son plays violin, so I know the instrument has only four strings. Then Jebbin explained five-string fiddles to me."

Jebbin swallowed the food in his mouth. "Hmm, yes. Told him all about violinists, and fiddlers wanting a hybrid violin/viola so they could have the low C to add some depth without losing their higher range on the E string. Isn't Archie's a Brunkalla, Emory?"

"Yep. Handmade right here in Illinois. Martin lives up near Chicago."

Chatty nodded. "That is good to know in case my Ragesh should decide he wants one someday. So, with that explained and filed away in my head, we went on. We are processing a good many things. The killer most likely wore gloves as no prints other than Dr. Dawson's were on his unusual fiddle or anything else, but scrapings were taken from the strings anyway to look for DNA."

"The wound strings in particular would hold skin cells well, I would think," I put in. Jebbin and Chatty both nodded.

"We have been running mass spectrometer and gas chromatograph analysis on the material in those three little pouches, as well as on the pouches themselves. Pass the garlic bread, please." Jebbin reached for the plate as Jason held it out to him. "Thanks. We could tell they're leather of some sort, but don't know what animal the hide came from yet."

"My guess is not bovine," Chatty interjected. "It is very soft and pliable. Delicate. Although I know cowhide can be made to be this way, I still think it is something else. And then, of course, blood and other fluids need to be analyzed. Antonia is quite certain the man was drugged. He was a big, strong man, and one would think not easy to strangle so neatly. She said the autopsy revealed no evidence he had struggled."

Chatty looked up at me. I think he might have been blushing, but it is hard to tell with his coloring. "Does this upset you, Emory? When I've eaten here before, we talked shop after the meal, not during."

"No, not really, though I appreciate your concern, Chatty." I looked down at my plate for a moment and took a couple of deep breaths. "Normally it wouldn't at all, but Archie was a friend, so it's not as comfortable as usual. You are all under a ridiculously tight deadline and I know you need to rush off again after supper. I want to know what's going on, so please, keep talking."

"There is, at present, not much more to say. We have some tentative results, but nothing I would want to draw a strong conclusion from. Do you, Jebbin?"

Jebbin smiled. "Well, I'm not the one doing any concluding. I merely observe and clean up after you on this case. That said, no. I wouldn't want to say much either. Hopefully by tomorrow afternoon, we'll start getting some definitive results. Particularly after we combine our conclusions with Antonia's." He looked over at Jason. "You've not said much, Jason. What news from the interrogation room? Or are you going to say you can't say?"

Jason flashed his sparkling white grin. "I could do that, couldn't I? Be funny after you two being more than willing to talk but not really having much to say yet. Good ole genial Henry and I took on the most likely suspects and the two hapless bystanders who found the victim." He nodded at Jebbin and me. "Based on our sources, who, by the way, Henry didn't want to acknowledge, we focused on Dr. Timothy Law and, as most anyone would guess, Mrs. Dawson."

"Um," Chatty mumbled around a mouthful of lasagna and garlic bread. "Yesh." He took a moment to swallow. "Yes, yes. Spouses are most always the prime suspect."

"Yep. Well done, Dr. Chatty. My respect for lab geeks goes up every day."

We all laughed and Jason continued. "Dr. Law had that nice argument with our victim. Which, by the way, Emory, his version of it had a different flavor than yours. His wasn't as tart. He told us he was drunker than he should've been and it was all a piddly rehashing of some old disagreements between him and Dr. Dawson." He winked at me. "Your version had a lot more spunk."

Jason sat back and stretched. "You have got to give that recipe to Diane. I am too stuffed, but happy!" He leaned forward, resting his beefy forearms on the table as he continued.

"Mrs. Dawson, well, she admitted she had come to the conference without her hubby knowing and that she intended to surprise him. I will say she seemed awfully surprised we knew about it. She said she had a couple glasses of wine with the meal and some kind of cocktail called a 'Pink Squirrel' during Dr. Dawson's talk, then a 'Grasshopper' during the first set of music, and was feeling 'simply too tired to listen to any more bluegrass,' her words not mine."

He nodded to Jebbin and me. "I've told you two you need to try something else. Anyway, she says she went outside to have a smoke in the cool air, thinkin' it might wake her up some, but decided to find herself some place other than his dorm room to spend the night. Called herself a cab, asked about bed and breakfasts, and he took her to the Victorian Lady. He musta sized her up good, 'cause it's the most expensive one in town. She says she went straight to her room and straight to bed."

"Sounds simple enough." Jebbin raised his eyebrows. "I assume there's some problem though."

"Oh yeah. It was nothing to call Denny at the cab company and check the run. The time the cabby picked her up was three thirty-three in the morning. *Not* right after the break between your music sets. So, she has a big problem."

We all sat there, thinking. There was still so much to figure out and only five days left to do it in. The guys all stood up at the same time, saying in unison they needed to get going. We all laughed over it, and Sophie and I walked them to the door. I then fed her some scraps before letting her out, cleared the table into the dishwasher, put the pans to soak in the sink, let Sophie back in, and finally went to bed. It had been a long day and I knew it was going to be a long, crazy week. I fell asleep to the sound of Hortense and Kumquat purring as they cuddled up at my feet.

CHAPTER 7

Rainclouds had moved into central Illinois during the night. Sunday didn't so much dawn as fade from the orangey glow of reflected streetlights into a misty gray scene from a hazy old black-and-white photograph. Leftover rain and the morning's condensation dripped from the trees onto our umbrellas as Jebbin and I walked to church. We were in our "Sunday-go-to-meetin'" clothes—a dress instead of jeans and a sweater for me, and Dockers, an Oxford shirt and sweater vest for Jebbin. I would have rather been in jeans, as my feet were getting damp in my nylons and dress shoes.

The various Jairus Twomblys down through the years were firm believers in freedom of religion, and the town they founded and grew bore the fruits of that tolerance. Jebbin and I happen to be Christians, Methodists to be precise, but the town included several other Christian denominations as well as active groups of Buddhists, Hindus, Jews, Muslims, Humanist/Atheists, and a smattering of others. One gets a lot of variety, even in a small town, when there's a prestigious college there. We mostly get along, but neither is Twombly a utopia. There are occasional problems among all the opposing points of view.

Jebbin and I sat in our usual pew in the large sanctuary; fourth from the front on the congregation's right side on the end by the windows. The altar cloths and vestments were still the white with gold symbols that go with the Easter season until Pentecost, which was next Sunday, when the cloths would all be changed to red. Reverend Hernandez knew about the murder, most likely all of Twombly knew, but somehow the fact that Jairus Aiden Merriweather Twombly VI wanted no hubbub about it was also known and so no hubbub was forthcoming. All she said was "prayer is needed for our church family at Twombly College and for the visitors there for the anthropology conference."

Sorry to say, other than the singing, I didn't pay too much attention to the service. My mind was busy with what I did, and didn't, know about the murder, and how I was going to get more information without getting myself in trouble with any of the powers that be.

We didn't have our usual leisurely, large dinner at the Cracker Barrel out by the interstate after church. Jebbin had to rush back to the lab. Instead, we had lunch with the Midwest Anthropological Studies Society conferees at Blythe Hall. If a conference went over a Sunday, Fiorello always put on a marvelous brunch buffet in the college cafeteria. Everything was offered; from breakfast items to a choice of dinner-type meats, vegetables, and salads. There was even a station for making sandwiches. Jebbin ate light (a sandwich) and fast (done in ten minutes) and left. To my great satisfaction, Timothy Law and I spotted each other as he was going through the line. Jebbin and I had taken a table for two, and I now flagged Dr. Law over to join me after he got his food.

"Hello, Emory! I'm glad we spotted each other. I'm not in a mood to be alone, but I really didn't want the same old chatter with the same old MASS people either," he chattered as he began to unload three heaped plates and a couple of small bowls off his tray. One plate had a cheese omelet, cheesy hash brown casserole, and a heap of bacon on it. Another had orange slices, strawberries, pineapple chunks, and three slices of cantaloupe. His breads plate held one of Fiorello's succulent large cinnamon rolls, a smaller caramel roll, two biscuits, and two foil-topped containers of honey. One bowl had oatmeal with cream and blueberries and the other had a third biscuit swimming in thick sausage gravy.

"Well, I hate to admit that I'm dyin' . . . ah, anxious to know what everyone is saying about the . . . about Archie." Lord, I felt so awkward about all of this. It's surprising how often we use expressions relating to death in one way or another. And I just didn't like how blunt the word murder sounded. "I'll do my best to not harp on it if you're tired of it all. I can imagine it's the talk of the conference whenever you all have some down time."

"Hmm." Timothy shook his head until he finally swallowed his bite of cheese omelet. "Not really." He looked at the plates and bowls in front of him and gave me an embarrassed grin. "I've gotten to know how your chef cooks and I hated to miss out on something, so I took a bit of everything along with my omelet, but I forgot to get something to drink."

He started to get up, but I laid my hand on his arm.

"I'll get it for you. I'm nearly done eating and could use a refill anyway. What would you like?"

"Coffee, black. Hate to admit it, but I'm a coff-a-holic."

I chuckled. "So is Jebbin. I like more variety. You tuck in and I'll be right back."

I returned with sweet tea for me, a leftover from my Southern upbringing, and black coffee for Timothy. I looked him over as I approached. His legs were bouncing under the table and he was eating with short choppy movements. Yet, his color looked good and his smile as he looked up was relaxed and natural.

"You said it wasn't the talk of the conference before I got up." I settled into my seat, put my napkin back on my lap, and picked up my fork. I finished my thought before I dug into what remained of my pot roast dinner. "I'm surprised. Are deaths common at your conferences?" I winked to let him know I was teasing. He grinned back.

"Oh yes! They happen every year. They usually send a note around asking for volunteers, but I don't remember seeing one this year. But Archie never liked to be passed over or upstaged. He probably wrote and insisted."

He was smiling, but there was a tiny edge to his words beneath it. He sipped his coffee, closed his eyes, sighed, and leaned back to enjoy the moment before continuing.

"Obviously, not really. I don't remember anyone *ever* dying during a conference. But no, it isn't the main subject of conversation. I don't know how to explain it, but most conversations I've been in on we've talked shop like we always do at these events. Who's out digging where. Who's research we want to hear about or read about. Who has an article or book out." Timothy ate a few bites and swigged down more coffee before he continued. "Which would, you'd think, lead us back to Archie. But it hasn't seemed to. I think everyone is uncomfortable and perhaps a bit scared. I'll admit, I'm a little frightened. After all, he didn't have a heart attack or something like that, and who knows what the motive was. Someone could have it out for anthropologists and, if so, we're all potential victims. Or it could've been just Archie.

"Mostly, though, if he comes up in the conversation at all, it's about the book. There is a certain amount of academic snobbery going on, I think. You know the sort of thing. All well and good he published a book, but not well and good that the general public has gone bonkers over it. It's almost as though it tarnishes the quality of academic work if 'normal folks' are able to read and understand it." His smile was crooked.

I nodded. "I've heard of that happening. Fame in one sector can lead to shunning in another."

"Hmm, yeah," he mumbled around another mouthful of food, then we both went quiet. I didn't know what he was thinking about, but I was thinking about how to ask what I wanted to ask without shutting him down . . . and without tipping my hand too much. He didn't need to know I'd been keeping an eye on him.

"The police and sheriff's department officers took me in for questioning." I stopped, rolled my eyes, blushed, and grinned. "All right. That sounded scripted."

He was laughing. "Yes. I was just going to ask which cop show you'd been on at the time."

"The thing is, they did take me into one of the library conference rooms and ask me questions. Have they talked to you? I mean, I'm assuming they are talking to all the conferees."

"Yes, they 'took me in for questioning' too. But I'm not sure I had much to say that was any help." He looked down at his plate, then up at me from under his eyebrows with a tight-lipped grin. "I have to confess, I didn't stay for your whole concert. No offense intended, but bluegrass isn't my style of music and I'd had a little too much to drink. The banjo was hurting my head, so I left at the break to go to bed." Timothy looked into my eyes. "Hope you aren't hurt by that."

I smiled and patted his hand. "No. I totally understand. There are styles of music that I can't take too much of myself. You weren't the only one who left early. Myra had pointed Archie's wife out to me earlier in the ladies', and I didn't see her after the break. Do you know his wife? Did you see her leave?"

Oops. The wall went up. I saw the new distance in his eyes. I'd overstepped my bounds.

"Yes. I know Mrs. Dawson. I knew her and Archie both when we were undergrads and she used to come to the conferences with Archie." He paused and his expression soured. "Until he started acquiring teaching assistants, that is. I haven't seen her in years, and I didn't see her on Friday."

I tried to backpedal. "I, I just . . . Jebbin and I didn't know her. We knew him from bluegrass festivals and she never came with him. I . . . didn't mean anything by it."

Timothy sighed and waved my apology aside. "Sorry. She's an all right lady; well, at least she used to be. As I said, I've not seen her in ages and people can change."

He stopped. He was looking everywhere in the room except at me. He *tunked* his fork up and down on the remains of his slice of ham. The table was vibrating from him jiggling his legs.

"I knew Archie in college. We, ah, roomed together the whole four years. Shared an apartment while getting our masters. He . . . he . . . Archie wasn't all he came off as being. He, ah, I mean he wasn't too horrible or I wouldn't have roomed with him all those years."

Timothy looked up, to heaven perhaps? He huffed as a wry smirk twisted his lips and shook his head.

"I wouldn't have gone into anthropology if it hadn't been for Archie. I was a language major. I was already fluent in Spanish and French, with a working knowledge of German. Archie had come in undeclared. He did some nosing around and found out that you can study just about anything and tie it into anthropology somewhere along the line. At first he was going to work on a sports emphasis in cultural anthropology, but then he got into fiddle playing and bluegrass music and heard about ethnomusicology and chose that instead. It was right after he first decided on anthropology that he convinced me that I should switch to linguistic anthropology."

He took some time out to eat, and then continued.

"But, yeah, old Archie did have issues, as we say these days. He was one person to those who knew him well and someone else to those who knew him more on the acquaintance level. But, I guess that could be said of most of us."

He dabbed his mouth with his napkin before wadding it up and tossing it onto his plate of leftover food. He leaned across the table. I leaned forward, too.

"I think I know who did it." He grinned and huffed. "Ain't that a hoot? Didn't tell the authorities because my evidence, if you can call it that, is circumstantial at best, but I think . . . yeah, well."

He stood up, picked up his tray, and gave me a small bow.

"With that, having said more than I probably should have, I will take my leave, Emory. I'm sorry I got a little touchy and ruined a good meal. Perhaps we'll have another chance to chat and it will be more pleasant."

I smiled my most reassuring smile. Not the easiest thing to do seeing as he was my main suspect, but I think I was convincing. "Not at all, Timothy. It's an upsetting business, one that is bound to stir up feelings of all sorts. I'd love to chat again."

He smiled. "Later then." He nodded, then walked away.

I sighed and turned my attention to my dessert. My fork stopped just short of piercing the chocolaty lusciousness as I thought of the cake's name. "Death By Chocolate Cake." Death again. The fork punched through, clunking as it hit the plate below.

"Ahem!"

My fork clattered against the edge of the plate as I cleared my seat, gasping. The sound had been insistent more than loud, cutting through my ruminations about deadly cake.

"I'm so sorry!"

A body moved into view across from me. Looking down at me was Dr. Cameron Garrow.

"I'm so sorry." She repeated with less volume and more concern in her voice. "I saw Dr. Law leave, so I thought you weren't opposed to sharing your table. There aren't many places to sit available. I was just going to ask if you would mind. I didn't mean to startle you."

A soft "hoo" came out with my exhalation. "Not at all. Have a seat. Dr. Garrow, isn't it? We met at registration on Friday but weren't really introduced." I held out my hand as she set her tray and herself down. "I'm Emory Crawford, a Twombly College professor's wife."

She smiled, taking and shaking my hand in a firm grip. "Yes, you remembered correctly. I'm Dr. Cameron Garrow, call me Cameron or Cam if you like."

"Cam it is then."

She was wearing another long dress, blended shades of browns, sleeveless and V-necked, with a light sage-green turtleneck underneath. Her hair was up. In a bun, I assumed, as I could see two bead-topped hair sticks peeking out from behind her head. Not all that different from my own outfit, though I was wearing a light blue dress, a white thigh-length cardigan, and had my hair in a French twist.

"You're too young to be a throwback to the 60s and 70s like I am." I nodded toward her dress. "We look like time travelers."

Her eyes twinkled with amusement. "I like the comfort of that era, but yes, I'm too young to have experienced it the first time around."

My cake needed coffee. After returning from the beverage station with that and tea for Cam, we gave our attention to our food for a while. The cake was melt-in-your-mouth succulent so there was no problem in making it last while she set to her quiche and fruit.

"What do you study, Cam? Your area of focus, I mean. Obviously, it falls under anthropology or you wouldn't be at the conference."

She took a small sip of tea before answering. "Revolutionary War era folklore."

That sounded familiar, though I couldn't think of why.

"Should be a lot of folklore in that time period. There was a great deal of old superstitions mixed in with people's Christianity."

"Oh my yes! They still used all the old medicines, or lack of the same. Much of it was downright magical in its approach. And, of course, they still sang all the songs and told the stories they brought from the Old World. They had old, strange laws and ideas of people's rights—or the lack of them—as well. It's fascinating."

"I bet it is."

We each paused to eat. I was having trouble holding myself back from turning my table conversations into something akin to the official questioning the law enforcement people conduct. My mantra ran through my head: What Would Jane Marple Do? I needed to be a nice motherly lady. Pleasant. Soothing.

"I wonder what those folks in the past would have done with the sad affair of Friday night?" I mused aloud, hoping it would be a gentle opening gambit. "There are some similarities, after all. The school is, in some ways, a small community and so are the attendees of the MASS conference. We do seem to be circling the wagons, what with Mr. Twombly's insistence on keeping things contained." I chuckled. "Well, I suppose 'circling the wagons' is more appropriate to the 1800s and the expansion west, but I'm sure there was something like that in your era of study."

"Oh, yes." Cam nodded. "The people in earlier times did circle the wagons if a group of them travelled together," she said finally. "If they were in a settlement or even in a city, they might have taken cover between a wagon and a building. Same idea."

"Yes! Exactly the same. You knew Archie, didn't you? I think I remember you commenting on him to Ms. Fordyce at the registration table."

I watched her carefully, but the question didn't seem to cause much reaction.

"Yes, I knew him about as well as most conference regulars knew him. If you attended very often, and I never have missed a conference, there was no way not to at least have an opinion of the man. Dr. Dawson was rather hard to be unaware of." Her lips quirked into a crooked smile. "He was a big man and he wasn't in the least shy or retiring. Some people socialized with him, some—even before his recent fame—fawned on him and others, like good anthropologists often do, watched his behavior from a distance. I was a mix of the first and last of those. I was sometimes in a social group that included Dr. Dawson, but I more often hung back and observed."

"I can understand that. We, my husband and I, knew him from bluegrass festivals, and I usually preferred to be an observer of Archie. Jebbin somehow enjoyed being more of a friend to him. But Jebbin has a way with fellow academics of all sorts."

Cam laughed lightly. "He must have, to have gotten close to Dr. Dawson." She sighed and shook her head. "Just my opinion I suppose. But then, one does hear things about colleagues that add to one's opinions."

Without looking up from my cake, I asked, "What sort of things?"

"Well, this would always come up when Timothy Law was being discussed. Supposedly Archie knew some things about Dr. Law that weren't very good. I only paid attention because Timothy always seemed the nicer of the two men. There are rumors about some kind of plagiarism while they were in undergrad. Maybe even grad school."

Her enchanting voice didn't fit the ugly subject. To me, she sounded as if she should be telling folktales about faeries and pixies.

"Timothy hasn't published many papers or journal articles and that can lead to people speculating on how that academic managed to get through school. Rumor was Archibald knew the sins of his roommate and helped keep it covered up. And then there are Dr. Dawson's affairs. Most of us knew about those, but some said his wife was fooling around as well."

Cam paused, glanced from side to side, and then leaned closer to me.

"Those could all be reasons to want Dr. Dawson out of the way. Who knows? Maybe Sonya Dawson and Timothy are an item and Archibald found out? I've read that spouses are always the first person the police look at in murder cases." That crooked smile came and went again. "If she has been with Timothy, maybe she'll plead the belly if they do accuse her of the murder."

Cameron's cell phone started playing music, cutting her off. She took the call, agreed to something, ended it, and snatched up her MASS tote. "I hate to ask, but would you mind bussing my dishes? They want me to cover one of the slots in the workshop schedule that Dr. Dawson was supposed to have. I need to hurry to my meeting room."

"I don't mind at all, Cam. Hope it goes well for you."

"Me too. Bye, Emory." She said the "bye" and my name over her shoulder as she hurried away.

CHAPTER 8

After bussing the dishes, I headed for home. I'd checked out those folklore books after my interrogation on Saturday but hadn't had time to dig into them. Soon I was ensconced at our dining table, open books and my laptop all higgledy-piggledy on the oak surface. Sophie had been out and back in and was now acting as a warm, furry footstool under the table. Hortense and Kumquat lounged on opposite ends of the table as though they were bookends, making sure nothing fell off while I worked. Well, nothing fell off unless one of them happened to bat it off, in which case it was fine with them.

The house around me faded away. I was transported into musty root cellars and old barns where the air smelt of horses instead of tractors. Bundles of herbs hung from low rafters. Corked and wax-sealed bottles sat upon narrow shelves and workbenches. Herbs and tinctures, concoctions and decoctions for protecting, for cursing, for healing and, yes, for killing, too, as most medicines that preserve life can just as easily take it. Most of them also had magical or mystical meanings and symbolism. I made notes of ones that caught my attention.

I looked at pictures of the people who knew how to grow, harvest, and prepare it all. Sometimes they were men but more often women. Some looked like average citizens, and others looked like the wizened witches and sly sorcerers from old etchings and woodcuts. I followed their paths from valued members of their societies to 'purveyors of evil' that society decided should be imprisoned or executed.

Church leaders and political power players came and went across the years, using or abusing these people for their own purposes, whether by seeking their gifts or seeking their deaths. Careers were made and ruined as the public's view of astrology, numerology, palmistry, and other methods of divination were manipulated. Many who hunted the practitioners of one occult art or superstition followed and encouraged others themselves. They pursued whatever would bring them the power they sought.

I stood in the shadows of Salem, Massachusetts, watching as writhing teenage girls chanted their neighbor's names. Twenty-five to thirty people, maybe more, died because of these girls and the fears of their elders.

My feet turned cold as I read about the "peine forte et dure," death by crushing, of Giles Cory. Then a black cat passed before my eyes. Goose bumps rose on my arms . . .

. . . And I was out of the book I was reading and back in my cozy house sitting at the dining table.

Sophie had gotten up, causing my feet to get cold, and Hortense, a mostly black cat, had walked across the book I was reading with that uncanny sense of timing animals have—just when it was time to prepare the chicken curry I was serving for an early dinner at five o'clock. The intensity of what I'd been studying tugged at me. I was loath to let it go. I toyed with the idea of telling the guys to go out for dinner, but then I would miss out on all their lab results, and I needed their information, even though I was pretty certain Timothy Law was the killer. I hoped they might find my information worth hearing, depending on what their scientific studies revealed. Jebbin and Chatty wouldn't be the only ones with information tonight.

With a sigh, I got up and headed into the kitchen. Good thing Sophie and Hortense have good intuition and had shaken me out of my reverie. Dinner would have been late otherwise and that wouldn't have been good, as Chatty and Jebbin wouldn't want to dally about waiting to eat. Not with the tight deadline they were working under. I took the thawed chicken breasts out of the fridge, gathered up the rest of the ingredients for the chicken curry, and got to work. Yes, it's pretentious of me to fix curry for an Indian, but I got the recipe from his wife, Deepti, and Chatty loved it the last time I fixed it for him. I got it all mixed and simmering, put the Basmati rice into my steamer, and then cleared my books off the table.

I was going to put my feet up on my chaise and was nearly there when my cell phone, which of course I'd left in the kitchen, started playing the introduction to "Cornbread Nation," a song by Tim O'Brien that Molly loves because it reminds her that her parents had Southern upbringings. I dashed back, plucked the phone off the counter, and swiped it.

"Molly!"

"Hello, Mum!" she replied in true British form. "Tomorrow you'll be Maman 'cause we'll be in Paris. Freddy has been to Paris lots of times and he's going to show me, well me and some others from the class, all over the place. Isn't that great! I'll get to see some of the real Paris, not just the tourist places!"

I jumped in when she paused for a breath. "Freddy?"

"Mum, he's just the nicest guy . . . er, bloke." She giggled. "He's English and has the loveliest accent, and he knows so much about art history from all over Europe. But he really loves American art. Can you imagine that? All this wonderful old art and he likes our relatively new stuff. I mean . . ." She broke off as I heard someone speaking in the background. "Mum? I gotta go. Freddy took me out for real London fish and chips and then we went on the best, he says, of the Jack the Ripper walks and we just now got to the Ten Bells to have a drink before we head back to the hostel. The Ten Bells is where they say a couple of his victims were drinking before he killed them. It's the actual same place. Isn't that too cool?"

"What time is it there, and you're out on a date with what's-his-name?"

I heard her say "just a sec" to someone before the background noise lowered and she spoke more softly into her phone.

"Yeah, Mom. A date! Isn't that the best? His name's Freddy, well, Frederick Edward Wilkinson, and he's so sweet, Mommy. He often says he's one of the few, from his initials, but he won't say the few what. He just grins and says that's for the other person to figure out. It's close on to ten at night. I gotta go, and don't worry, we're only having one drink, sort of in honor of the women that The Ripper killed, then it's back to the hostel. I love you, Mommy!"

My phone went quiet, but my mind did not. The conversation was pure Molly when she's excited. Fast with few pauses. And a date? With someone she'd only known a few days? That wasn't very Molly at all. Not that she's never dated or anything, but she's usually the sort to go a tad slower than that. I smiled, dispelling some of my concern, when I thought of her calling me "Mommy." Even though she's twenty-two, she still calls us Mommy and Daddy from time to time—usually when she's missing us or feeling low. Obviously, she wasn't feeling low, so it was rather nice to know that in spite of the fun she's having, she was missing me like I was missing her.

Taking my phone with me this time, I finally made it to my cozy chaise to contemplate Molly out with Freddy, following the trail of Jack the Ripper to the Ten Bells.

Chatty closed his eyes and sighed, finished chewing his mouthful of chicken curry, then spoke. "Nearly. This is nearly as good as Deepti makes. Nearly. I have found that cooking resembles chemistry in many ways, but still it is an art, not a science, and two people can follow the recipe exactly and yet their dishes will not be exactly the same. It always amazes me."

I felt myself blushing. "Thank you, Nibodh. I really do think being raised in the culture makes a difference, and I've never lived the Indian culture, though I do love your music, jewelry, clothes, and some of the cuisine."

"True, most correct. Deepti cannot make fried chicken the way you do. But, as you say, you have lived the southern American culture. It is the same with research and development chemists, I think. The art of it, I mean. They have to have the . . . knack I think it is called. They have the knack of making the chemicals do new things. We, on the other hand," he gestured at himself and Jebbin, "if we play too much we might ruin the validity of the evidentiary results and a criminal goes free."

"Exactly! And thus you have given me a perfect segue, Chatty. What have you two, well mostly you I realize, discovered in your evidentiary tests?"

He smiled his charming smile. "I'll let my humble observer tell you. I want to eat your most excellent curry before it turns cold."

I looked at Jebbin and shoveled a forkful of curry and yogurt/cucumber salad into my mouth to let him know I wouldn't jump right in with an interruption. He shook his head and grinned.

"I guess I have the floor, then. Good thing I was eating while you two were chatting. Well, let's see. Where to start? We know who did it."

My eyes went wide with surprise, both at what he said and that I hadn't either choked on my curry or sprayed it all over.

"Yep. DNA on the fiddle strings. Fingerprints on the fiddle. Yep. A jealous fiddler. Jason and Henry will be here to arrest you in just a few minutes, Emory Mary Crawford." My husband stared me down, all seriousness and business, before grinning like a fool.

I swallowed my curry. "Ha. Ha. You're soooo funny, Dr. Crawford. And anyway, you two told me last night there were no fingerprints other than Archie's, so you blew it with that. OK. Now what did you really find out?"

"Nothin' nearly that exciting, though we did find out some things.

There was no DNA on the strings other than Archie's. And, as mentioned on Saturday, no fingerprints on anything other than Archie's on his belongings. So, our killer is not an idiot."

Jebbin looked at Chatty. "It still amazes me with how long fingerprinting has been around and, actually, how long DNA testing has been around, that there are still so many crimes solved because the criminal leaves one or the other or both."

Chatty nodded, a forkful of curry pausing short of his mouth. "True. Very true. It is indeed amazing. Continue." The curry found its way home.

"So, yes, neither of those to help us out. No fingerprints on anything. Well, other than the ones that were supposed to be there. Toxicology work is still in progress both at our lab and the pathology lab. He was clearly drugged. Let's face it, he was a big guy, he should have done some damage to his attacker. But there's nothing. No skinned knuckles or anything. Tox screens for the usual suspects haven't shown anything yet, so we're both starting to look for the unusual.

"The amulets are all the cheapy sorts of things that are sold at medieval fairs and shows catering to role-playing gamers or various Neo Pagans. Nothing unique or traceable. We are having some surprises with the three little pouches." Jebbin leaned in to whisper, "For one thing, the leather is cat skin."

I did choke on my food this time, coughing it out into my napkin. Chatty handed me my glass of water while Jebbin patted my back. I recovered and squeaked out, "Cat?"

Chatty nodded. "Yes. Jebbin and I hope we will not upset Hortense and Kumquat with this news. You are all right now?"

Now I understood the whispering. Not upset the kitties. Ha. I suppose it was a touch of humor to help dispel the creepiness of the discovery.

"Yuck!" I made a disgusted face and sat back, away from my food. "Just . . . yuck!" I paused to cough. "Cat?" I asked again.

"Yep." Jebbin shrugged his shoulders. "*Felis silvestris catus*, domestic cat. And don't ask how our killer came by it, we've no idea. Cat leather isn't readily available."

"Although," Chatty put in, "I think it quite possible someone took a dead cat they claimed to be their own to a taxidermist and requested the cat be preserved with some small sections of the skin to be tanned into leather."

I must've looked like I felt as he quickly added, "It was the nicest possibility that came to my mind."

"Yes, it isn't too bad I suppose. I can think of many possibilities, Chatty, and none of them, including that one, are normal." I wanted to get off the subject of cat skin. "What was in them? Were you able to find that out yet? I mean, I remember, Jebbin, you said the techs opened one that night at the garden and found plant matter in them, but have you figured out what kind of plant matter?"

Chatty gestured for Jebbin to fill me in while he got up and helped himself to more curry.

"We ran samples through the gas chromatograph and the mass spectrometer, which showed right away that the pouches had some toxic plants in them. We asked Celia Miller to have a look at some of the larger fragments to see if she recognized anything as a botanist. There were a few things she recognized for certain and several things she suggested from the GC/MS readings. Some weird stuff."

Jebbin turned toward the kitchen. "You've got the info in your satchel, Chatty."

"Yes, yes. I do. One moment."

He hustled back into the dining room, his plate full of curry, yogurt and cucumber salad, topped off with more asparagus, green beans, and julienne-cut carrot vegetable medley.

"I should not eat this much, but I cannot resist. It is all wonderful, Emory. I will tell Deepti how well you have cared for my stomach. She will be pleased."

"Thank you, Chatty. Glad you're enjoying it so much."

He set the plate down, and then bent over to dig around in his satchel. I tugged my own notes from under my placemat.

"Plants. Plants. Where are the papers on the . . . Here!" He waved them over his head as he sat down. I think he was going to hand them to Jebbin so he could get back to eating because he started to reach toward Jebbin's place, only to find that my husband was following his example and was in the kitchen getting seconds.

"Um. Let us see." He looked at his full plate with longing, then with a shrug turned his attention to the papers in his hand. "We have . . . ah, <u>Podophyllum peltatum</u>, <u>Succisa pratensis, Cuscuta, Ferula asafetida, Aralia spinosa L</u>, and <u>Buglossoides arvense</u>."

"Let me see," I interjected. "That would be mandrake, Devil's-bit Scabious . . . um . . . oh yes, dodder, which is also known as devil's guts, devil's hair, devil's ringlet, hellbine, and witch's hair. Then we have devil's dung and devil's walking stick and the last one is corn gromwell aka devil's stones."

Both men stared at me.

"What?" I barely managed to hold back a smug smile. "I've been doing research."

"Obviously." Jebbin smiled. "But how did you come up with all of those? Makes you look a little too 'in the know' if you take my meaning."

"I . . . oh!" I felt my face heat up from something other than the curry. "Oh! No, no. I obviously didn't know ahead what was in those pouches. And no, I've not been spying on the lab. I just figured since the amulets had devil-related meanings and so did the bouquet of dried flowers at the MASS registration table on Friday, that . . ."

"What bouquet?" Jebbin leaned in toward me like Kumquat pouncing on a mouse.

I jerked back against my chair. "Th-the bouquet on the registration table. I . . . didn't I mention it to you, or, or Jason or someone?"

"No." He leaned back, closing his eyes and huffing.

Chatty spoke up. "How often do they empty the large trash dumpsters here? Might this thing still be in one of them?"

Jebbin looked at his friend and colleague, weariness suddenly showing in the creases between his brows. "Yeah. Yeah it should be. Note paper, Emory?"

I hopped up and got a pad of paper and a pencil off the hall table where I'd stashed my books and things so I could set the dining table. I set them down beside him and sat back down. "I'm sorry, guys. I really thought I had mentioned it."

Jebbin wrote *look for bouquet in the Hall's dumpsters* on the pad. "It's OK, hon. Really. You're not a detective, ya know. It should still be there, though it might be soggy since it's been raining." He looked at me. "What about the arrangement?"

"Ah. It had plants in it that had good portents. Like, um, good luck charm-type plants. Things they used in the old days to keep evil away. Cam, Dr. Cameron Garrow that is, she noticed. Well, she would. Her field of study is pre- and Revolutionary War era folklore. They, the people back then, even if they were Christians, they would still have those plants around to ward off evil spirits. I even knew the meanings or uses for most of them once she mentioned it and I took a better look."

"Well, we best see if the police can find it anyway. It might tie in."

We all stared at the table in silence. The mood of the dinner, a time of sharing food and camaraderie, had dissipated. I don't think any of us felt like eating any longer.

"I'll put your plates in those dish carriers I have for taking stuff home from church pot lucks and you can heat them up later in the microwave in the faculty lounge," I muttered as I rose to gather them up. "Cept the yogurt/cucumber salad. I'll put that in something else so it stays chilled."

"Thank you, Emory. I am sure I will want some later," Chatty said as I took his untouched plate.

Jebbin called Jason Anderson and let him know some officers

would need to go dumpster diving. The guys left. I cleared the rest of the table, put away the leftovers, and started up the dishwasher.

I wandered into the living room and spotted the copy of Archie's book, *The Devil's Music: Murder and Mayhem in Western Folk Music*, lying on the table by my chaise. Why not? I really should read the dumb thing. I fixed a mug of tea, then plopped onto the chaise to read. I was part way through the preface when I realized I hadn't told Jebbin and Chatty about my certainty that Dr. Law was the murderer. Between the shock of the cat skin pouches and my flub with the bouquet, I'd clean forgotten to play my trump card.

"Ah well," I said aloud to my pets who, as usual, had gathered around their mom, "I'll let them know tomorrow." I started reading only to stop again. "Tell them what about the bouquet?" I'd said that it had anti-devil dried plants in it, that it bothered all of us. "That's not much, Miss Marple, old dear." The great thing about talking to your pets is that they don't add cars to your train of thought that end up sending the whole thing onto a siding. I was free to voice my thoughts and keep them on the track I wanted them on. "Ok. Myra hadn't brought them. She showed Cam and I the pathetic arrangement she'd brought that was probably the same arrangement she's brought to every conference. So . . . where did the creepy one come from?"

If I'd been a cartoon, one of those cute little ecologically incorrect, old-style light bulbs would have appeared over my head. I looked anxiously around for my phone, which of course was in the kitchen where I'd left it while tidying up. I scooted my rear out of the chaise, got my phone, and called someone I should have thought to call sooner: Aine McAllister. Aine, a good Gaelic name pronounced Awn-ye, was the thirty-something owner of Mysterious Ways: Plants, Herbs & Irish Blessings, a lovely shop just off the town square in Twombly's historic district. She owned the building and lived in a spacious, open layout apartment above her business.

"Hello?"

"Hi, Aine, this is Emory. Sorry to call you after hours but I have a question I need to ask you."

"No bother at all, Emory, m'dear. What'cha needin'?"

"Did you get an order for a dried flower arrangement to be delivered to the college Friday morning?"

"Yes. For the registration table of the conference the murdered man was involved with. It was a very interesting arrangement to guard against manifestations of the devil and his web of evil. Not the usual request for a conference; well, except perhaps for that alternative beliefs conference last Halloween at the Holiday Inn by the interstate. But even that one wasn't nearly as interesting; they wanted black and orange mums, black and orange carnations, and thirteen Black Magic roses. Black Magic roses are gorgeous! This order was a lot more fun to put together even though it apparently didn't do its job very well."

I grinned. Aine always went straight to the heart of things. "Exactly. I was there at the college welcome table and, despite the fact that it creeped me out, I did think it was rather original. Can you remember who ordered it?"

"Yes. Albertha Moses. The order came in the mail, in cash, three weeks ahead of the date the conference started. Albertha listed each plant she wanted represented and their meanings, though I already knew all that. I was told to have at least one of each and then extras of whatever was easiest to get to bring it up to the amount she sent. The return address was only Owl Creek, North Carolina and a zip code."

"I wouldn't think you get many orders like that, you know, cash in an envelope and being so particular about what's wanted."

"Especially the cash. Lots of folks are picky about what's in their arrangements. I will admit, as soon as I touched the envelope it gave me odd vibes. I said a rosary over it and cleansed it with sage smoke." She paused. "Why are you asking after it?"

Ah, Aine. Mysterious Ways was more than the name of her shop. It was the lady herself. She went to mass every Sunday, but also would do something like saying a rosary over an envelope then cleansing it with the sage smoke used by many Native American tribes. Though firm enough in her Christian beliefs, she was in tune with alternative healing and mystic ways of dealing with anything that might give a person the willies.

"As I said, I was there. I saw the arrangement; it was lovely by the way. Creepy but lovely and it just seemed weird. It bothered a couple of other ladies there too. I just got to wonderin' who might have sent it and, well, if you'd gotten the order or if it'd been sent your way from one of the other shops. I can't imagine any of the other florists in town knowing what to do with such an order."

"That's for sure!" She laughed heartily. "Nope. Pots & Posies and Floribunda Fantastique both call me for the more curious orders. They're great for the normal plants and flowers, but they don't do much with dried arrangements, and they aren't into the old terms, meanings, and uses for herbs and weeds, let alone do things like put together herbal teas and tonics for people. I am listed with Teleflora and FTD, and the listings show that I do herbals and specialize in dried plant matter, so I usually get the orders right off. I'm sure that's how Albertha got my address."

"Speaking of which, can you do up another order of the tummy tea for me. I just can't resist some of the things I know my stomach rebels against. That and this, ah, death has me stressing out."

"Will do. I'll set it aside for you. Just come by when you can."

"Thanks, Aine, and thanks for the information about the arrangement."

"Any time, Emory. Hug all your critters for me and tweak Jebbin's beard."

I hung up and moseyed back to the chaise, taking my cell phone with me for a change. Soon the cats and dog were asleep, and I was reading Archie's book.

The hazy red numbers on the DVR showed eleven fifteen. Kumquat was kindly holding my place in Archie's book by lying on the open book on my lap. I'd managed two and a half chapters before dozing off. I nudged Kumquat off the book before swiveling my legs over the side of the chaise and hoisting myself up. She sauntered into the bedroom. I wobbled after her, turning off lights as I went—except the one over the kitchen sink so Jebbin would have some light when, if, he came home from the lab.

I had some time while doing my pre-bed routine to think about Archie's book. After reading the preface I was rather impressed. In it, Archie talked about when he fell in love with bluegrass music and the stories it told. How he followed the trail of bluegrass back to Bill Monroe, back to barn dances and the people of the eastern American hill country, to the flatlands and coastal areas where the Scots-Irish music had met the spirituals of the slaves, blending in their African tunes and rhythms to eventually become American folk and bluegrass music. And always there were the stories the songs told. Stories about every part of human life since it began.

Archie then spoke of western Europe where explorers, merchants, and common folks looking for new lives left to see what lay over yonder across the wide oceans. All across Western Europe people were coming to begin anew—and they all brought their stories in songs.

But why murder songs? Why songs about crimes and criminals? Archie's answers were: Songs had been a way to communicate news and events, a way for people to express and experience feelings of anger without committing murder themselves. They expressed a community's sense of outrage if the criminal wasn't caught and their sense of justice if he or she *was* caught. They explored the reasons and emotions of criminals, such as rejection, lucre, lust, loathing, and even love. Or perhaps because songs about crimes also make good tales to tell and his book would tell the tale of those stories.

From there the book was divided into sections, with the first being an overview of murder songs in chapters one and two. Chapter one dealt with why murder songs are still popular, and the second chapter discussed categories of murder songs.

I would be rereading those chapters as little of what I'd read tonight seemed to have stuck, or maybe I was just too tired. Apparently, I'd faded in and out of awareness more than I'd thought. I finished with my bedtime prep, turned out the bathroom light, and bid my day adieu.

CHAPTER 9

I'm sniffing a dandelion, sticking my nose into it until its multiple petals tickle me. It smells odd, so I move it away to look at it. It looks like a normal dandelion, but my nose keeps tingling. Rubbing my nose, I bump into something cold and damp.

I jerked out of my dream and opened my eyes to find two huge cat eyes filling my vision. Hortense's whiskers had been tickling me, not a dandelion. My startle didn't bother her in the least. She sat there with the look of a mother getting her kid up for school.

"Meow-oooo," she announced with an emphasis on the "oo" that she sometimes adds to the end of her meows.

Translation: *Good morning, Mom. Get up and feed me my morning treat.*

Cats say a lot in one meow.

"Yeah, yeah. Pesty cat. You're a pestilence, you know that don't you?" She arched up, purring as I stroked her from nose to tail, then gently head-butted my forehead. "All right. I'm awake. I'll get up, Intense Hortense."

In the bathroom, Kumquat interrupted her licking of the drips from the bathtub faucet long enough to look up at me and add her squeaky soprano meow to the conversation. Sophie ambled in to remind me she needed to be let out. I smiled around my toothbrush as I thought about our bathroom as such a center for social activity.

Pre-dawn light shone through the window above the café curtains on the bedroom windows. Yesterday's clouds had moved on; it was going to be a sunny day. The leaves of the maple outside the window still looked dark gray instead of green, but the house wren was already singing from his post in the branches around the wren house. I breathed deep then let out a sigh. Oh yes. This was a take Sophie for a walk kind of morning, not a stay in my jammies morning. I pulled my jeans from the drawer and balanced on one leg at a time as I pulled them on. Good to practice balancing, I feel, instead of always sitting down to put my pants on. A bright yellow T-shirt from a bluegrass festival, socks, and my blue-and-white flowered Converse high-tops completed my look. Sophie went into the backyard to attend to her business while I fed the kitties their morning canned food treat in the screened porch. When Sophie was done, I hung my camera around my neck, shrugged into my Worsham College of Mortuary Science hooded sweatshirt, stuck my cell in my pocket, went out, and made her sit while I put on her harness and clipped on the lead; then we headed out the gate toward the campus.

I gulped in deep lungfuls of early-summer-flavored air. Mornings like this were made for breathing. Fresh washed air. Earth scented air.

This is what green smells like.

One nice thing about living on the edge of the campus was how suited it is for walking a dog. There are sidewalks and the paths that years of student's feet have worn across the lawns. There are large open areas where the kids play Frisbee and touch football during the school year that are great for giving Sophie off-leash runs. And when the running is over, there are the various gardens with benches for catching our breath.

We went west, away from the low angled rays of the rising sun . . . and away from Fountain Garden. I hoped Archie's death wouldn't put me off that garden permanently, but for now the details were all too fresh.

If we stayed out long enough, perhaps the light wouldn't be in my eyes on the walk back. We left footprint trails through the dewy grass of the West Field; mine going fairly straight while Sophie's drew a filigree of curlicues.

Archie's book had been off to a great start, I thought, plugging back into my thoughts from last night as I walked and kept an eye out for any birds or flowers to take photos of.

The first section, with its overview of murder songs, was reappearing in my mind. Chapter one pointed out that many of the early reasons for murder songs were still with us. We still needed a way to communicate news and events, but now it wasn't so much the dispersal of information that we got from songs as it was a delving into the reasons, emotions, and thoughts of the killers or their victims. And, people just like hearing mystery and murder stories. As with horror stories, we don't want it happening to *us*, but there is this fascination with things that frighten us.

The second chapter dealt with the various categories of murder songs. Men murdering women. Women murdering men. Parents murdering their children or children murdering their parents. Murder because of love. Murder because of hate. Killing for profit. And, well, is there an end to things we humans can use as "reasons" to kill? Like the song, "Down in the Willow Garden" (also known as "Rose Connelly") where one way the lyrics can be interpreted is that the murderer kills Rose because his father encourages him to with the statement,

"That money would set me free
If I would murder that dear little girl
Whose name was Rose Connelly."

I'd wandered about West Field nearly as much as Sophie while distracted with my thoughts. The sun had risen but was still low, casting those long shadows I loved so much, because at least my shadow got to be tall and slender. Just ahead were the Japanese Gardens with their peaceful surroundings. Perfect for the rest of my thinking.

"Sophie! Come on, old girl. Let's go to the garden."

She stopped nosing around and chasing birds to look at me.

"Come on."

She galloped toward me, stopping suddenly in the traditional"dog wants to play" pose; front legs flat on the ground and rump, swaying along with her tail, up in the air.

"No, daft dog. I don't want to play chase the doggy. Come here and we'll go to the garden. You can drink from the pond, you know you like that." I pointed to the Japanese Garden.

Sophie pranced around, did the play pose again, and then trotted off where my finger pointed. I smiled, chuckled, and followed her. I went around the southern end of the huge stone wall that forms the eastern end of the rock garden, following after Sophie along the sloping wall and through the small arched entrance.

I breathed deeply of the moist scent of dewy sand and rocks, my eyes soaking in the beauty of this other world.

That is part of the purpose of Japanese-style gardens, to draw you away from the everyday world and into a world that looks totally natural but is really the result of careful design to bring serenity to the people who enter it. The one on Twombly's campus is a long, narrow rectangle running east and west, but you don't realize that when you're inside it. The large stone wall I had skirted before passing through the portal is covered with ivy on the outer side. A couple of deciduous trees and a few shrubs keep it from standing out starkly on the college grounds. Inside the garden, you're at the foot of a small cliff. A stream of water sparkles down its face, occasionally falling a foot or two to form small waterfalls before ending up in a small pool, creating the stream that runs from one end of the garden to the other.

There are four entrances into the garden along each of the long sides, two that enter the Zen garden and two that enter the planted garden. The easternmost end, where the cliff is, is the rock and sand part of the garden—what most people would call a Zen garden. Its rocks and raked sand, as you walk westward along a meandering path, meld into the planted garden farther on, where the stream ends in a pond. Rock walls slope downward from each end of the cliff wall to be replaced with wooden fences as the Zen garden merges with the plants. I turned and looked toward the western end where trees frame an opening that shows Elder Hill ten miles away. It's the highest point in Golden County and the highest hill in the high ground known as Prairie Hills.

I wandered along the paved walkway. Traditionally a tarmac-paved path would be improper in a Japanese style garden, but today accessibility is more important, and I'm glad for it. I walked up the slope of the rough wooden bridge that crosses the stream nearest the rock garden and stopped midway to watch the swirling red, orange, yellow, black, and white shapes of the koi swimming by. The breeze is softer here, carrying the muted melody of toned wind chimes from the west end of the garden and the clinking of the bamboo chimes that hang from the bridge. Leaving the bridge, I strolled on, seeing the essence of the ocean in the raked ripples of the sand and enjoying that same peaceful openness one feels at a beach. Gradually, sand-loving plants appear, including prickly pear cactus and agave that are planted in inconspicuous containers that the school's Japanese gardener, Masaki, puts in the greenhouse during the winter.

The day was starting to warm up, so I unzipped my hoodie as I passed through evergreen bushes and then onto the second bridge. I paused to look at a turtle bobbing along, body below the water's surface and head sticking out to catch a breath, when I realized I hadn't seen Sophie lately. A chill touched the breeze, although no cloud had blocked the sun. I chose to ignore it.

"Sophie? Ya in here, girl?"

A whimper came from the rock garden behind me. Turning, I saw my big gold dog at the far side of the rock garden, in the gloom of the long shadows at the base of the cliff. She was sitting on the raked sand beside a stack of wood and rocks. Sophie looked at me, whimpered again, and then lowered her head as she looked back down at something at the edge of the pile.

"It's okay, Soph. I'm coming." Once I got to where the sun wasn't in my eyes, I looked carefully at the rock garden and noticed a bunch of the smaller rocks had been taken from their places and dumped onto what looked like a sheet of plywood. Despite the rocks having been moved, the only prints in the pattern-raked sand were Sophie's. I stopped where the green grass ended, not wanting to mess the pattern up any more than my dog already had. The air was chilly and damp in the shadow of the stonewall cliff.

"Come on, girl. Just some work being done on the garden. Come on now, before you mess up any more of Masaki's raking job."

Sophie whined and pawed at the ground near a rock that had fallen off the plywood, then looked at me and woofed.

"I know, I know. 'Come quick! Little Timmy's fallen into the well!' But there's nothing here but a pile of rocks on a piece of . . . ply . . . wood."

I hesitated. There was something not quite rocklike about the rock at Sophie's feet.

CHAPTER 10

"Mrs. Crawford?"

I didn't startle at the distant calling of my name; it filtered into my thoughts gently.

"Uh-huh."

"Mrs. Crawford?" The voice was closer now.

"Yes. Yes, it's me Masaki." I spoke louder this time, recognizing his midwestern voice tinted, like one of their delicate traditional watercolors, with a Japanese accent.

"What is Sophie doing in the garden? She usually knows better." He drew up beside me, arm extended, forefinger pointing at my wayward dog.

"She's not happy with something by your pile of rocks on the plywood."

He shook his head. "Not my pile of rocks, my board though. But it was over in the Chisen-Kaiyu-skiki part of the garden. We were using it to hold a wheelbarrow load of mulch and a few plants that were ready for transplanting. It shouldn't be here."

He followed up his perplexed tone with action, striding out onto the rippled sand toward the pile of rocks and Sophie. I watched as goose bumps rose on my arms and the hairs on my neck started tingling. Let Masaki check it out, I wasn't going anywhere near it.

He patted Sophie on the head as he looked down. "You're okay,

Sophie. You're . . . Oh my God!" Hand to mouth, he backed away until he was only a foot or so away from me at the edge of the sand. Eyes wide with shock, he turned to face me.

"In *my* garden, this time! How could someone do such a thing in *my* peaceful garden, Mrs. Crawford? In a Zen garden, for goodness sake!"

"Do what, Masaki?" I had one of those "rabbit ran over my grave" shivers. I knew it was a dumb question the moment I asked it. I think I'd known the answer since I heard Sophie whimper as she stood in the oceanless ripples of sand at the base of the cliff.

"There is someone under the wood and the rocks. The face is . . ." He swallowed hard. I knew just how he felt. "It is swollen and – and discolored, but it is a face, a person's face, not a stone."

I nodded while I pulled out my cell phone.

It came to life, playing my nonspecific ring tone. I stared blankly at it a moment or two before answering.

"Uh . . . hello?"

"Emory?"

"Yes. Jairus?"

"There is another one, isn't there."

The man was spookier than my own intuition ever was. "Yes, in the Zen garden. Sophie found it. Masaki is here too."

"I'm almost there. I was out for my jog and didn't like the look of the Japanese Garden this morning. Had the feeling you and Sophie went for a walk with the weather having changed, and I know you like that garden, so thought I'd try your number. Call Jebbin and Dr. Chatterjee. I'll call Detective Anderson and Captain Schneider."

He hung up without saying goodbye. I disconnected, then called Jebbin. By the time he picked up, Jairus had come into the garden through the hill and pond garden's north portal and was coming down the path toward Masaki and me.

"Hi, hon!" My sweetie sounded chipper considering how tired I knew he must be. "We got some good information from Antonia and Celia . . ."

"I've got some bad information."

There was a pause. "Oh?"

I took a deep breath and let it out slowly. I was starting to feel shaky. "Jairus wants you and Chatty in the Zen Garden immediately. There's another . . . another body."

"On our way." I heard the tired resolve in his voice before he hung up.

I hung around and watched this time as the sheriff's and police departments did their thing. Sophie and I stood on the weathered wooden bridge, my hoodie off my hips and hanging over the railing, close enough to see without seeing too many details. Just yesterday I had been reading about the Salem Witch Trials. Just yesterday in my cozy home, I'd read about Giles Cory. Now, Masaki's peaceful garden had been desecrated by the same grotesque "peine forte et dure" form of execution.

I have to admit, it was fascinating watching the forensic team start at both entrances to the Hiraniwa garden and work their way in, thoroughly searching the tarmac path and the grassy verge on either side. That done, they formed a long line and moved abreast onto the sand, inching their way across its gentle ripples, leaving them storm-tossed in their wake, until they reached the grim machine of death.

They removed the stones one at a time. There was no need to hurry. There was no life to be saved. Each one was bagged in the white trash bags the teams brought with them and tagged like any other evidence would have been. No telling what the murderer might have left on them. The board was carefully lifted and wrapped in plastic.

Dr. Antonia Conti then stepped forward and knelt to do her job as medical examiner and forensic pathologist.

Jebbin and Nibodh Chatterjee had followed well behind the forensic team, only walking on the ground the team had already covered. They're the lab guys. They don't gather materials at the site as that could be seen as a conflict of interest—a chance to tamper with evidence. A few minutes after Antonia knelt beside the victim, Jebbin stepped away and came over to join Sophie and me on the bridge. It was even more important that he stayed away from the gathering of evidence since he is an employee of Twombly College.

He slipped his arm around my shoulders and pulled me close.

"I hung around over there just to see if they could make an ID," he explained. "Like Archie, all his stuff is in his pockets. It's Dr. Timothy Law."

"What!" I pulled back to look up at him. "No! It can't be Timothy. He-he's the

m-murderer."

"Was that the conclusion your sleuthing led you to?"

I nodded.

Jebbin looked across the crime scene to the base of the cliff. "Somehow, Emory, I don't think he was."

My gaze followed his. Antonia's assistant was getting the body bag laid out. I turned around to face the Chisen-Kaiyu-skiki end of the garden and let out a sigh. I leaned into my husband and reached up to hold onto his arm that was now in front of me.

"No. I don't suppose he was."

"The good news I was going to share when you called would have burst your Miss Marple bubble anyway. We finally figured out the readings on Archie's tox screen. Well, Antonia and Celia did. He was poisoned with passionflower. Highly toxic stuff. They determined it was mixed into the wine and the cheese spread that was in his stomach. The murderer must have reckoned Archie'd be thirsty and hungry after performing, and they wouldn't have any trouble getting him to take the stuff. A real double whammy putting it into two consumables. He . . ."

I twitched and Jebbin hesitated.

"I want to go home, hon. Will you walk me home?"

"Sure thing." He used a finger to turn my face toward him. "I can't stay though. You know that, right?"

I nodded.

"Chatty!"

"Yes, Jebbin?" I heard Chatty's melodic voice reply.

"I'm taking Emory home. I'll meet you back at the lab."

"That will be fine, my friend. May I suggest we order dinner for all of us from that excellent Italian restaurant that is here in Twombly? Gulotta's I think it is called? I think your good wife would be happy to not cook dinner tonight."

"Sounds good. Honey?"

"Hm. Guess so. Just wanna go home."

"We'll do that," Jebbin answered as he turned to face the same way I was. "See you in a bit, Chatty. Come on Soph."

With his arm around my shoulders once again, we all headed out of the garden toward home.

I hadn't felt this dirt-poor awful in ages.

Poor Timothy! Not only did I feel terrible because he was dead, but I felt even worse because I had thought he was a murderer. Who did I think I was? So much for being Miss Marple.

I started to fix some toast. Even though I wasn't hungry, I knew I ought to eat. Coffee. I needed coffee, too. I quickly set it up and hit the switch. The luscious aroma filled the kitchen only to be overpowered by a stench. The toast was burning in a toaster oven gone mad. All the elements were glowing a fierce red and I scrambled to pull the warm plug out of the outlet.

The toast was toast. I threw it out and turned to get a bowl out of the cupboard. I'd have cereal instead.

I heard splashing behind me. Jerking around, I saw I hadn't put the coffee pot in place and coffee was merrily cascading out of the under-the-cabinet coffeemaker onto the counter and onto the floor.

Forget the coffee. I shut off the coffeemaker and mopped up the mess.

I gave up.

I wandered around the house for a while, looking at my furniture, paintings, photographs, and knickknacks, but not seeing any of it. I could hear my dead mother's voice in my head.

"What did you think was going to happen? Did you really think you'd solve a crime? It's just like everything else you try. You get all gung-ho and think you can do it all and then screw it up. You didn't finish college. Couldn't seem to have a career at anything. You're just lucky Jebbin managed to work and was happy with a homemaker for a wife."

I shriveled under the accusing voice from beyond the grave, just as I'd shriveled under it when she was alive. My mom had sure had a way with words. I crawled onto the chaise, wrapped the comfort of the afghan my dad's mom had made for me when I was a teenager around myself, and cried.

I cried for Timothy, who had been so friendly and polite to me the first morning of the conference. I cried for Archie who, even though he was obnoxious, didn't deserve to be murdered. I cried for myself. I felt alone, idiotic, and useless.

And why hadn't Molly called when she had more time to talk? What was going on over there? Didn't she know I . . .

No. She didn't know her mother had gone off half-cocked again, thinking she could be something special or important. I hadn't told her about Archie or Miss Jane Marple or that her mother was having delusions of grandeur.

That last bit was juvenile, like something my mom would have thought, and that sobered me up a little. One by one, Kumquat, Hortense, and Sophie added their comforting presence to that of Grandma's afghan.

I quit crying and just stared at nothing while my mind descended into familiar negativity.

The critters and I all jumped out of our respective skin and fur when the rattle of keys in the lock and the front door opening announced the arrival of Jebbin and Chatty. It was a good thing they got carryout, because I had been completely lost in my depressing reverie.

"You feeling any better, hon?" Jebbin looked over at me as he waved Chatty around him toward the dining table. "We got the big chef's salad you like, chicken Alfredo, and spaghetti with meatballs." He stopped and came over to the chaise. "You aren't feeling any better, are you?"

"No."

I could see him thinking. "Mom in your head again?"

"Yes."

He held out his hand. "Up ya get, old girl."

That made me grin a small grin. He's called me "old girl" since we were first married. I took his hand and he helped me up.

"We are going to eat delicious food from Gulotta's and you're going to have some of your favorite oolong jasmine tea and a glass of wine, and then I'll draw a warm bath for you before we spend the evening together in front of the TV watching the movie of your choice."

I plopped back down on the chaise in shock. "You're going to be home?"

He smiled and nodded.

"But, but . . . but the case! It's even worse now, and I'm sure Jairus still wants it solved by the end of the week. How . . . ?"

"Ah, ah, ah! None of that, Mrs. Crawford," Jebbin chided.

"I would not stand for his working tonight."

I looked at Chatty, who winked at me as he set our places at the table, then at Jebbin and back again.

"He needs to be with you tonight. I will take no arguments. I could tell where his heart is, and it is not at the laboratory. His sense of duty made him argue with me that he needed to stay but, no, I will not hear of it from him, nor from you. We are at a point where everything is, how to express it? Steeping. Like tea. A time that we wait. I am more than able to keep an eye on the few things that will be ready later this evening since Jebbin is only able to observe anyway." He smiled his bright, charming smile. "The plans for your evening, however, are entirely his own."

Jebbin helped me back up. I went straight to Chatty and gave him a tight hug.

"You're a sweetheart, Dr. Nibodh Chatterjee."

He returned my hug. "Yes, I am most certainly a sweetheart. Deepti tells me this frequently."

We all helped get the food set out, dished up our plates, and set to eating. It was wonderful. Even though I still wasn't as hungry as I should have been, not really having had anything but a bowl of cereal around lunchtime, I ate more than I thought I would. Knowing I'd have my dear hubby home went a long way toward lightening my mood. I even decided to ask how the work was going.

"You really want to know?" Jebbin eyed me with concern. "It won't get you all down again?"

"Hmm. I guess I won't know until you get into it, but on the other hand, I'm curious."

It was good to see Jebbin's smile light his eyes. "You are always curious. It's one of the things I love the most about you. All right. Well. We heard from Jason. Henry snubbed me as usual, but Jason called just before we left to get dinner. They brought in the conferees for questioning again and got a rather different story from Archie's wife, Sonya, this time. Although it doesn't really clear her for Dr. Law's murder, she admitted that Timothy was with her the night her husband was killed. They had a fling in his dorm room. First time, she claims, even though she made no attempt to hide that, yes, she'd had other affairs once she found out that Archie was dabbling. But, other than saying she never left her room at the Victorian Lady, she didn't have an alibi for last night. So, she's cleared for one murder but not the other."

"Mm. Unless they did the first together and she then decided to . . ." I couldn't seem to keep my mind from hatching plots, even though I was still uncomfortable about the two deaths.

"That occurred to the authorities as well," Jebbin assured me. "Jason said they have a few people under surveillance and she's one of them. They don't really have enough evidence to hold anyone. Just a lot of suspicions."

"And," Chatty interjected, "it is thought the same person committed both murders as the occult theme is present in both. I have been told that form of killing, the weight upon the chest, was used in the famous witch trials here. The ones that happened in . . . where was it you said this occurred, Jebbin?"

"The Salem Witch Trials in Salem, Massachusetts." I answered for my husband. "I was actually reading about it yesterday afternoon. They only used it on one man, Giles Cory. The rest were hung. They used it on him because he wouldn't give a plea of either guilty or not guilty. It was a way to extract a plea or a confession, and I guess it often worked. Mr. Cory never confessed."

Chatty nodded, his eyes looking sad and distant. "Yes, it does not surprise me, what you say Emory. All cultures have been brutal and many still are brutal. India no less than any other. It is very sad."

We became lost in our own thoughts and the conversation dwindled. Chatty finished his chicken Alfredo and salad, took his dishes into the kitchen, and took his leave of us.

Jebbin drew a bubble bath for me while I went into our room to take off my clothes and gather up my comfiest pajamas, then he cleaned up while I soaked. Afterward, we watched *You've Got Mail* with the furry "kids." The movie was soothing; it made me think of loves and lives lost, of not wasting either while we have them. And at the end, when Joe and Kathleen meet in a beautiful flower garden, it did my soul good. I needed a reminder of garden goodness and how love can heal hurts. Then, for the first time since this all started, Jebbin and I went off to bed together, shutting the door behind us. The "kids" could find their own entertainment.

CHAPTER 11

I woke with a jerk. I'd been dreaming of running through endless gardens, all of which had a dead body or two in them. The bedclothes were a mess and the cats were nowhere in sight, which was unusual. Normally I barely move during the night and wake up with at least one cat somewhere on the bed with me. I drew in a deep breath and let it trickle back out. I could still smell the pillow spray I like to use when Jebbin and I are in the mood. That breath and the scent helped the fright from the dreams dissipate.

I looked at the clock; 6:02 changed to 6:03 as I watched.

Last night had been an oasis of comfort in the midst of the current nightmare. Flipping the covers back, I slid out of bed and trudged into the bathroom.

I shuffled into the kitchen, where even the smell of coffee and a warmed cinnamon roll didn't really cheer me up. I let Sophie out, fed the kitties, and took my breakfast out to the table on the screened-in deck. The not too cool but not too warm morning air helped my mood a bit. The songs of robins, wrens, and cardinals blended with my wind chimes like environmental meditation music. Hortense and Kumquat joined me to perform their after-breakfast cleaning in the fresh air, while Sophie seemed content to roam around the yard and have brunch later.

Halfway through my cinnamon roll, which despite my gloom was luscious and gooey with the butter I'd spread on it, I looked at my dog happily romping after a squirrel and realized she had the right of it. Although I couldn't stop feeling the loss of two people, I didn't need to wallow in it—nor in my failure to figure the whole mess out.

I should do something.

My cell phone rang.

It was playing "Foggy Mountain Breakdown," a classic banjo instrumental and Jebbin's ring. The phone was in the living room, so I made a mad dash and caught it just before it went to voicemail.

"Good morning, hon."

"You're up. I'm glad. I didn't want to wake you."

"Up, dressed, and out on the deck having breakfast. Had to run for the phone, though. I forgot to take it out with me."

"The media knows about the murders."

He just popped it out with no leading into it, stopping me short in my thoughts.

"The media knows? Even with Jairus insisting they not be brought in yet?"

"I know. Maybe the Twombly Touch is fading or maybe it was easier to keep one murder under wraps, but not two of them." There was a pause. "Sorry, Emory. I'm being blunt. Scientist mode. Too much work and not enough time mode. Well, a lot of work for Chatty at any rate. I think that's bugging me, too. I'd rather be working instead of observing. Jairus still wants it all solved by the end of the week, though this time he did add, "If at all possible." Not exactly permission to ease up, but it helps to feel a little less pressured. Are you okay?"

"I'm . . . yeah. Okay. Last night helped a lot."

"Yeah. For me too."

His tone warmed me through and through.

"At any rate," he continued, "I want you in the house this morning. There isn't as much media as there could be. I'm sure Jairus has kept it to a minimum, but I'd still like you out of sight. I think it's being kept quiet that you were around when the . . . when Archie and Dr. Law were found, but my name and Chatty's are sure to come up, and most everyone knows you're my wife. I don't want them trying to wheedle information out of you. I think Jairus is gonna try to have them gone by noon. Well, at least off campus. I don't think he can make them leave town. This isn't the Old West where the town boss can order someone outta Dodge."

We both laughed. We both needed it.

"I'll stay put."

There was quiet as we both mulled the situation over. I usually didn't mind being home. I love home, that's part of why I'm a homemaker. Jebbin usually loves his lab, that's part of his love of chemistry. But none of this was normal. Being told to stay home is different from *staying* home, and being told not to do lab work is different from observing because you want to.

"Home for lunch?" I asked.

"Mmm. We'll see. If yes, I'll bring something. Unless you . . ."

"Bringing is fine."

"I'll let you know before I, or Chatty and I, show up. Wouldn't want you to think the press is storming the gates."

I smiled at the smile in his voice.

"Love you, Dr. Crawford."

"Love you back, Mrs. Crawford."

We hung up and I felt better. Oddly enough, in some strange way it felt better that the media was here. Two men had been murdered. That mattered. It was important to their memory that it didn't seem swept under the rug.

And Jairus Twombly VI still wanted it all solved by the end of the week.

Phone in hand, I started for the screened porch—or deck, we used the terms interchangeably—when Archie's book caught my attention. I picked it up.

"*The Devil's Music: Murder and Mayhem in Western Folk Music.*" I read aloud. "Who knows, Archie, you may end up in one of those folk songs someday because of all this."

I started to chuckle, then stopped. The devil's music. The devil. Both murders had elements of old superstitions, witchcraft, and the devil. Maybe there was some connection to the book? Maybe the murderer felt Archie needed to die by his own words?

The book went with me to the porch. It was seven thirty in the morning.

I had no interruptions till Jebbin called at noon.

"Hi, hon."

"You sound distracted. Am I interrupting something?"

"Hm? Oh! No. Well, I'm just reading Archie's book is all." I glanced at the clock facing out of the kitchen window. "Oh, it's lunch time. Are you coming home?"

"Yep, though I can't stay long and Chatty won't be coming. Jairus is more on edge than he was before, understandably, so Chatty's going to keep plugging away. But this not seeing you is getting to me. I'll order some sandwiches from Jimmy John's and hopefully get home before the delivery guy gets to the house. If not, can you cover it and I'll pay you back?"

"I can. Get some chips and an oatmeal raisin cookie for me, too, please. You know my favorite sandwich."

"Yes ma'am. That's a number eight, 'Billy Club,' on seven-grain bread, add onion and Dijon mustard. Can I get you a pickle with that, ma'am?"

"Oh yes, please!" I laughed. "And extra cheese."

"Yes, ma'am. We'll have that to you before that weird chemistry professor, banjo-picking husband of yours gets halfway home."

"Just see that you do, young man."

Mixed in with his beautiful laugh, Jebbin said goodbye, listened to my goodbye, and then hung up.

He got home just as the delivery guy was walking up our front steps.

"Sho," Jebbin started to talk around a bite of his "Italian Night Club" sandwich, changed his mind, chewed, swallowed, and began again. "So, you said you were reading Archie's book?"

I finished my own bite of sandwich. "Yes. I'm about two-thirds through it. Well, two-thirds not counting the appendices, index, and such at the back."

"And?"

"Better than I expected."

Jebbin grinned. "You were expecting it to be bad even though it made the bestseller lists?"

"I've read many a 'bestseller' that didn't impress me."

"What's in it? What does it deal with?"

"Murder and mayhem in western folk music," I smugly quoted the title.

"Ha, ha. Very cute. Now, how did he cover his chosen topic?"

"He covered it with hard covers and a rather attractive paper dust jacket." I held my hand up to stop Jebbin from saying anything else. "I'll stop, I'll stop. It is well organized and well written. In the first section, second chapter he divvies murder songs into different categories or types and then in the following three sections, each chapter deals with one category as applied to the section heading. The categories or types are . . . hang on, I'll grab the book." I got it and came back to the table, pulling my chair around to the same side so I was sitting next to Jebbin. "Here, you can see them for yourself. Murderer gets caught and feels remorse. Murderer gets caught and feels NO remorse. Murderer gets caught and we don't know if he/she felt remorse or not. Murderer does NOT get caught—we don't know if he/she is remorseful and is never punished. So, Section two is "Songs Based on Actual, or Presumed Actual, Murders,' with chapters three through six covering those kinds of songs by the four categories. Section three is "Songs Based on Fictional Murders," and "Section four is "Songs Based on the Wrong Person Being Accused, Tried, and Punished for the Murder."

"Wow!" Jebbin pulled the book closer to himself to flip through its pages. "I'm actually impressed."

"I know! Who'da thunk? But all that aside, he must have had a great editor." I almost snickered. "I can't imagine Dr. Archibald Finlay Dawson not dropping famous names at least once in every chapter. You know how he was at jams, always going on about, 'When I jammed with Vassar Clements. When I jammed with Stuart Duncan. When I jammed with Tim O'Brien, or Tex Logan or Chubby Wise.' And Lord only knows if he actually did jam with any of them." I shook my head. "There's been a couple of times in the book where he mentions talking with someone, interviewing this or that person, but that's it, and even that is presented in a straightforward manner. *Not* at all what I'd expected."

"Hmm." Jebbin gathered up the papers from his Jimmy John's and headed for the trash bin. "I see your point, but I also think you're right that it was probably his editor's doing. They know people get tired of a braggart. Plus, this isn't just a bluegrass book, and a lot of people probably wouldn't be impressed by those names anyway."

"True. Very true."

I hadn't even finished the first half of my sandwich when Jebbin came over and kissed the top of my head. He'd inhaled his sandwich and poured his soda down his throat.

"I'm back to watching Chatty have all the fun. You want us to bring dinner in again?"

"Sure." I smiled my broadest smile. "You know I never turn down the chance to get out of making a huge mess that I have to clean up, much as I do love cooking. But really," he looked like he needed some reassurance, "just tonight. I'll go back to cooking tomorrow."

His face relaxed. "I'm saved. I'm not sure how long I could survive without home cookin'. I'll call before we head over."

I picked up Archie's book from where I'd set it off to the side of the kitchen table since I wouldn't be reading while Jebbin was home, found my place, and started reading.

At two fifteen I was finished.

Good thing the library was still open. I went out the door and locked it behind me. I hoped the press was gone as Jebbin thought they would be, but it didn't matter. I just had to talk to AnnaMay, my best friend and the head librarian. I walked as fast as I could to the Hall.

CHAPTER 12

I rushed into the Hall's main entrance, through the foyer, across the wide main hall, and up the broad central staircase. I hustled through the huge doors and turnstile. Directly ahead, facing the entrance, is the main desk. I scurried around the end, nodded a greeting to the startled student volunteer there, and shot straight into the office of the head librarian.

"Who's dead now?" AnnaMay Langstock glanced at me before looking back at the paperwork on her desk.

"No . . . one. No one . . . new."

"Then why are you all disheveled and hyperventilating?" She took a longer look at me this time before waving her hand at an empty chair. "Sit. Compose yourself. Then tell me what you're in a tizzy about." AnnaMay went back to her papers. She could be so frustrating at times.

I sat.

I composed myself.

I tossed Archie's book onto her desk.

AnnaMay calmly turned it to face her. Where my friend got her placid, centered personality, I don't know. I've met her parents and they're both flighty types. Maybe it was the eight years AnnaMay spent in the Air National Guard that had done it. My waif-like friend looked as though basic training should have killed her, but she always spoke highly of her training and years in the military.

I reached over to tap the book for emphasis. "It's all wrong."

"You know the information in it is false?"

"No, not that, though it might be. I wouldn't know about most of it. No, it's the feel of it. The, ah . . . voice of it. It doesn't sound like the Archibald Finlay Dawson I knew."

"Hmm." She ran a finger around the edges of the book before picking it up, hefting it like she was trying to figure out how much it weighed, staring at it like a psychic doing a reading. "What are you inferring? Ghostwriter? Plagiarism?"

"Something along those lines, yes."

Her right eyebrow rose and dropped back down with the nod of her head.

"Authors don't always write how they speak. Their books don't necessarily carry the author's personality. That's part of being an author, giving the books a life and voice of their own."

"I know. I know. I've taken enough creative writing courses in my years here at Twombly." I felt my perplexity showing on my face. "But Archie was pompous and arrogant to the nth degree. There is simply no way it wouldn't come through in his writing." I tapped the book again. "This just doesn't sound as if Dr. Archibald Finlay Dawson, braggart bluegrass fiddler, wrote it."

"Who do you think did?"

I huffed out a chuckle. "That's exactly the question. Who? Well, back it up a bit. *Did* someone else actually write it and if so, who."

AnnaMay set the book down and laid her hand atop it. "You strongly suspect the former, yes?"

"Yes." I nodded. "And I think that could be the motive for his murder."

"And the other fellow? Dr. Law. How would his demise fit into your theory?"

"I don't know. I hadn't thought that far head." Plots of the mysteries I've read floated about in my mind till one rose to the surface. "If Timothy, Dr. Law that is, didn't kill Archie over the book, he might have known whom Archie stole it from, and that person may have killed both of them. There are rumors, long standing rumors, surrounding the two of them; that Timothy plagiarized while they were in undergrad and grad school. They were roommates through their bachelors and masters studies."

"Hmm." My friend closed her eyes. I could sense her taking it all in, sorting it all out.

"I came over here to ask if we could get our hands on copies of Archie's and Timothy's masters theses or doctoral dissertations. Or both. We could compare the writing styles and see what we get."

AnnaMay turned to her computer. After a few seconds she asked, "Where did they go to school for their masters and doctoral degrees?"

That stopped me in my tracks. I was sure Archie had mentioned his schools, couldn't remember if Timothy had mentioned his. "Not sure either one of them mentioned the where. I only know that both the bachelors and masters were from the same place."

"Not hard to find out." She tapped keys as she spoke. "All of that information should be listed in their faculty bios." She flipped open Archie's book. "It should say in here where he teaches. Um . . . not on the front cover flap. Here, on the back one. Prairie Grass State College in Ottawa, Kansas."

Another blow to my Miss Marple-ness. I should have thought of all that.

"Do you know where Dr. Law taught?"

I knew this. I'd heard it somewhere. C'mon brain. I visualized a computer with the little pop-up that says, 'searching . . .'

"Yes! Thank you, brain. He teaches, eh taught, at McGarvy."

Key tapping followed, then finger tapping as AnnaMay's computer took its time finding the schools' websites.

"Here we go. I have both college sites up, and the college of choice for our recently deceased college professors was Western Michigan

University in Kalamazoo. It should be no problem at all to obtain their masters theses. For doctoral degrees, I've got University of Texas, Austin for Dr. Dawson and . . . University of Missouri-Columbia for Dr. Law."

I nodded as I made notes on my phone. "We know Archie studied ethnomusicology. What did Timothy specialize in?"

"Cultural . . . wait a minute."

AnnaMay took her hands from the keyboard, running them through her sandy-blond-gray hair before fixing me with the look I'm sure she used when she was a supply officer and some airman didn't have the proper paperwork for his request.

"Why am I doing this for you instead of Jebbin or Dr. Chatterjee?"

"I'm helping them since Jairus wants this solved so fast."

"Ha. I almost believe you. You're playing at amateur sleuth, aren't you?"

It doesn't help when your best friend also knows your reading habits. I could feel my cheeks heating.

"Sorta. Kinda. All right, yes. But they both know about it and I am sharing all my info with them."

She stared me down a few more moments before shrugging.

"Why does this not surprise me? Just tell me all about it when you can. I'm assuming that for now it's all top secret and confidential."

"Sorry to say, I think it has to be, yes."

"And I thought the military was bad. People have no idea what goes on at colleges and universities." She looked heavenward, then looked at her computer. "Cultural anthropology. Dr. Law's dissertation was 'The Foibles and Folkways of the Mountain People of the Missouri Ozarks,'" She looked at me over the top of her computer glasses. "He would have run into old devil superstitions studying Ozark folkways."

"Yes. Yes, he would." I shivered.

AnnaMay's eyebrow rose again. "Rabbit run over your grave again?"

"You know me too well. You're even using my granny's old term for it."

She just grinned.

With a start, I realized what we were talking about. I leaned across her desk.

"Wait a minute. How'd you know about the devil aspect to all this?"

"What books did you check out on Saturday?"

"You weren't here!" I exclaimed, then slouched back in my chair and stared at the ceiling. "Why do I always forget, you are the great and powerful wizard of the library. Fair enough, back to the case. Dr. Cameron Garrow knows about devil stuff too. Ms. Myra Fordyce might, as well, from her studies of Hutterites. Archie may have known some of it as well via the folk music. In fact," I tilted my head to look at AnnaMay, "most any of the attendees could know about occult symbolism, superstitions, and folklore. Even if it isn't their specialty, it could be a personal interest, and we'd never know unless we ask them directly." My head flopped back down.

"Well, my dear friend, you are welcome to sit there as long as you wish. I'm going to be calling these schools for copies of the deceased's papers. I think it is an excellent idea to pursue, and I may as well take advantage of one of the perks of my job."

This time when I looked up, I was grinning. "Nobody will think it strange for a college librarian to call and ask for copies of academic papers."

She flashed me a conspiratorial grin. "How soon do you need them?"

"Yesterday would have been good, but if they could send them electronically or by courier, today as soon as possible would be wonderful. Jairus wants the case solved by Thursday."

She closed her eyes, waved her hands over her computer while muttering, and then turned to me with mischief glinting in her eyes. "The Wizard of Twombly Library will do her best."

"Good. This Miss Marple wannabe will head back to her staid home to brew tea and consider who all the suspects in this affair remind me of. Have a student run anything you get over to the house."

She tossed off a salute, which I returned even though she wasn't looking at me as I left her office. I sauntered out of the library, sashayed out of the Hall, and moseyed on home. No one accosted me. If the media folks were around, I didn't see them and they didn't see me. A robin sang in a maple, a jay cawed from the top of an oak. If you didn't know what had happened here in the last few days, you'd never guess it. Twombly College appeared to be its usual bucolic self. I saw a few MASS attendees, recognizable by their ID badges, walking along sidewalks and paths. Some were skipping talks or hadn't any scheduled as they lay out in West Field, their MASS tote bags beside them. They wore various styles of warm weather dress, either starting to work on this summer's tan or avoiding sun on their skin with long sleeves and pants, but enjoying its comfortable presence.

Feeling lighthearted for the first time in days, I crossed Rigel Boulevard and started up our walk. There was something on the porch. I climbed the steps. A black trash bag had been tied closed with red ribbon. A white tag dangled from the ribbon.

Okay.

Now what?

Gingerly I lifted the tag so I could read it.

You'll understand this.

I thought about it. If I'd understand whatever the bag contained, that meant I could look at it and not be instantly killed or there wouldn't be time to understand. It must not be a bomb, then. Could be something poisonous, however. Hmm . . .

I decided to open the bag right there on the porch.

Take a good breath.

Pull the ribbon.

Pull open the bag.
Step away fast.
The tops of dried plants poked out of the opening.

CHAPTER 13

Gasping, I moved away from the bag. Great! More dried flower arrangements. Although the one at the Midwest Anthropological Studies Society's registration table had been good plants, in that they were for keeping the devil away, the whole thing was still part and parcel with the murders. Dried flowers no longer thrilled my soul.

It hadn't blown up. No strange dust wooshed up as the bag opened. I moved back to check the other side of the tag, which I should have done to begin with, but let's be honest, I wasn't thinking calmly at the time.

"*You'll understand this,*" the front still proclaimed, giving me another of those eerie shivers as I flipped it over.

"*This is bursting with good luck, blessing & protection that I think we all need just now.*
Your new friend,
Myra"

Peeling back the bag, I saw yellow yarrow, sweet peas, rosemary, hyacinth, bay, and bittersweet. Three shafts of bamboo and a spray of plume grass at the back gave support to the arrangement. Yes, a nice florist's arrangement. The business card for *Mysterious Ways: Plants, Herbs & Irish Blessings* was on one of those plastic cardholders they always poke into flower arrangements. That explained how Myra had gotten hold of so many dried flowers and how she knew they were "good" ones. The things in my bouquet, a separate card informed me, gave: courage, friendship, blessing, happiness, protection, hex-breaking, healing, and an increase in psychic powers.

I reckoned the lot of us, conferees and locals alike, could use all of it.

"Mrs. Crawford?"

I was bent over the arrangement looking at the cards and nearly crashed head first into my front door. I looked under my outstretched left arm at the upside down people standing at the foot of the steps. They were as big a shock as the black plastic bag had been. Straightening, I turned to greet my visitors.

"Naomi, hello. And Mrs. Dawson. I . . . ah, we've . . . um, never met, but you were pointed out to me earlier . . . ah, in the ladies room the night of the opening banquet. My husband and I are sorry for your loss."

Okay. What were they doing here? No. What were they doing here *together*?

"Thank you, Mrs. Crawford."

Naomi had been the one to startle me. Sonya had a rich, elegant contralto voice. A fine dark chocolate compared to Naomi's youthful peppy Skittles.

"Call me Emory."

She nodded. "Sonya." Her smile was lovely, but weary.

"Won't you both come in? I have ice tea, rosemary lemonade, sodas, ice water?" Good grief! I'm babbling! Turning to open the door, I collided with Myra's gift, caught my balance, scooped it up as gracefully as a junior high boy at his first dance and led the way into my home. Sonya wanted iced tea. Naomi took a sparkling water. I had lemonade, hoping the tartness would cut the sense of the surreal.

Out on the screened porch we sat down and stared at each other. "Emory, we . . ." Their voices blended nicely as they spoke in unison.

Naomi took charge.

"Emory, we know this must seem really weird to you, Sonya and I showing up on your doorstep together."

"I've long known my husband wasn't faithful." Sonya cut to the point. "I had observed Naomi from the back of the room during the dinner. She wasn't draped all over Archie like most of his *'teaching assistants'* usually were. I came upon her today, sitting in the garden where . . ."

"You know," the current TA whispered.

"I know." I nodded my head.

"I don't know why, I just felt I could talk to her. Should talk to her." The women looked at each other as Sonya continued. "Imagine my surprise at finding her to be an intelligent young lady."

They chuckled, and I joined in.

"I know. I had the same surprise at our table during the banquet. First impressions and book covers don't always tell the whole story."

Naomi blushed. "I totally expected Mrs . . . Sonya that is, to hate me. You know, one of those huge catfight scenes like they have in those reality TV shows that aren't really real. I was surprised when all she wanted was to understand. To find out if Archie had ever talked about her and maybe said something about why he felt he needed to play around."

They reached for each other's hands and held on tight.

"But he hadn't. Not much, at any rate. He told me he was married, occasionally grumbled about his wife. That was all. He . . ." She looked at her feet in their ankle socks and athletic shoes. "The trip here was the first time he started putting the moves on me. Like what you just said, Emory." Her head came up. Dignity showed on her usually perky face. "Archie figured I was a stereotypical cheerleader, like in all the bimbo movies, even though he knew I was an A - B student. He just assumed I played the game. And I did once. My senior year in high school. I started school late because of my birthdate, so I was legal age, and the orchestra director and I had a fling. You two don't need the details. It ended hard and nasty and, for me, that was the end of a lot of innocence. I've been cautious ever since when it comes to dating, and wary of older men."

We sat and soaked that in. It fit in with my impressions of Archibald Finlay Dawson.

Sonya's smooth voice broke our meditative spell.

"I never really knew why he did it. His ego was all I could ever come up with. That and the machismo ideal of the best man having lots of women. I don't deny, I've had a couple of short affairs." I watched a tinge of red creep up her neck. "I got lonely and spiteful. Figured why should he have all the fun? Fun. Ha!" Her lips twisted. "They weren't all that fun. I haven't had anyone for . . . well, several years now."

Kumquat meandered onto the porch and sat right between Naomi and Sonya. She's my comfort cat; she always knows who needs something soft. The widow scratched her ears, the almost other woman massaged her shoulders, the cat purred.

"When we were first married, he was great. We were great. I went to bluegrass things with him. He went to art shows with me. We laughed a lot. Then, about four years in, it just stopped and never came back."

With a touch of panic, she drew her gaze back from the mid-space she'd been staring at.

"I don't mean we didn't interact at all. We did. We still talked and went places; I only stopped coming to these conferences about five or six years ago. We still had sex. But I could tell; Archie wasn't totally there with me. Eventually I found out he was dallying. I made the decision to just put up with it. My parents would have looked harshly on a divorce, even for infidelity, and my family is my rock. Oh, the decisions we make." She went back to staring at nothing.

"But," I couldn't resist, "you slept with Timothy Law that night."

"Dear sweet Timothy." A wistful look flitted across her features chased away by sorrow. "We were both drunk and mad at Archie. At the time it seemed the right thing to do. We were both embarrassed the next day and didn't even want to admit it to give ourselves alibis." She slowly exhaled. "I feel worse about Timothy than I do Archie. I'd long expected Archie to come to a bad end. I'd never heard anything bad about Timothy, yet I had the feeling Archie had something over him. I never found out what. I think Archie knew something that Timothy couldn't risk having revealed."

Our home phone interrupted Sonya, and I scurried off to answer it.

"Emory. It's AnnaMay. Dr. Dawson's and Dr. Law's masters theses should be in your email inbox. Dawson's dissertation will be here later tonight by courier, I gave them my home address. I thought it might be a good idea to keep you and your house out of it. Law's dissertation will be delivered to the library tomorrow morning at 9:00 a.m.."

I started to jump with excitement but remembered the ladies in the sunroom could see me.

"Bless you!" I hissed. "Can't talk loud now, but bless you!"

"You owe me, Crawford. See you at nine tomorrow."

Without hanging up the phone, I looked at the clock. Nearly four. I peeked at my guests. I needed to get information out of them or get them to leave, one or the other.

Or both.

And I would call Jebbin and tell him I didn't feel up to having him and Chatty come for dinner, would they mind catching something at the lab.

I had thesis papers to read.

After I got rid of my guests.

I hung up the phone. "Sorry about that," I said as I headed back onto the porch.

Naomi and Sonya waved my apology off.

"So. Are you both suspects?" Okay, blunt, and I already knew the police were following Sonya. But if they had information to give me, I wanted it.

Oddly, it didn't seem to offend either of them.

"Yes." Naomi frowned. "We can't leave town and I know I'm being watched." Turning to Sonya she asked, "Are you?"

"I think so. I've . . . I've not made an effort to notice. Hadn't thought about it, to be honest. I'm just so on edge." She looked at her fingers as they crimped what had been a crisp linen skirt.

"I didn't kill Dr. Dawson." Naomi quickly filled the conversational void. "I mean, I suppose I'd say that even if I had, but I didn't. I'd only known him a few months, and he'd been nothing but businesslike until this trip, and even here he hadn't overstepped his bounds to any degree that could have inspired . . ." Her turn to pause. "I never met Dr. Law until the conference. What reason would I have to . . ."

Sonya picked up the thread. "If I was going to murder Archie, I would have done it years ago when he started having his affairs and our marriage became a farce instead of a romance."

She looked up, fire glinting in her eyes.

"We would have taken a trip to Greece and something could have been arranged there where I have a lot of family and they have a lot of connections."

The light in her eyes mellowed. The proud tilt of her head relaxed, and she smiled.

"You see, I thought about it once upon a time. Oh, yes. I thought about it a great deal. And then I thought, why? Why should I risk my own neck for his? I'd worked while growing up, so working again didn't frighten me. So, I've worked. I have my own company, investments, and money. I have my own circle of friends. It's rather like being single and sharing one's house with a roommate who has privileges. When needed, we play the part of a moderately happy two-career couple most effectively. And I most assuredly would not have hurt Timothy. He was one of the few old friends from Archie's and my early days that I retained. Even though I rarely spoke with him, when I did I could be completely honest with him as to what was happening in my life. I ... I regret his loss more than my husband's."

We sat there. Birds sang and chirped in the trees.

I believed them both.

For whatever reason, I was convinced Archie was killed for something to do with academics, not sexual passions. Someone, past or present, had a more professional grudge. A professional passion. And believe me, I've witnessed some long-standing grudge matches that could and did erupt into brawls over such matters. There is hate, envy, greed, and larceny galore behind the academic screen of respectability.

No.

Hamlet said the play was the thing. For me, the writing was the thing. Maybe not the book. Maybe something that had been festering since years past. But I was willing to bet the farm that I was about to find out that there was a long trail of Archie's writings that didn't sound as if he'd written them.

"Well, I hate to say this, but Jebbin and the forensic scientist that has been brought in on the case to prevent conflict of interest are going to be here about six o'clock for dinner."

Naomi popped up. "Oh! It is getting late. We really should be going."

Sonya rose. "Yes. Thank you so much, Emory, for giving us some of your time. For being willing to listen to what we had to say."

"My pleasure. I hope it helped some."

Surrounded by the patter of pleasantries, I walked them to the front door.

CHAPTER 14

At last Sonya and Naomi were gone.

Much as I hated to, I called Jebbin and asked if he and Chatty could have dinner at the lab. I could hear the confusion and concern in his voice, but he didn't argue the matter. Just said okay, told me to make sure I ate something, told me he loved me, I replied in kind, and we hung up.

I got my laptop, a big mug of iced tea, and got ready to do a lot of reading. Sophie padded onto the porch, wanting out, which I obliged. Hortense and Kumquat floated up to the top of the table on the side opposite the computer. They tucked their legs under and wrapped their tails around themselves so that they looked like loaves of bread with a cat's head at one end and waited for me to settle into my chair. Okay, I know cats don't float, but if you've ever seen one jumping onto a bookcase or table top, you know what I mean. It looks effortless. I waited till Sophie was ready to come in, then sat down.

I downloaded both files and opened them in MS Word. Archie's had the earlier turn-in date, so I started with his.

His title was *The Social Significance of Wealth in the United States in the Twentieth Century and How It Relates to Music.* How totally Archibald Finlay Dawson. His wealth had defined him and obviously had defined his point of view in his chosen field of study.

It was fifty pages of well-written information about all the wonderful stuff the wealthy contribute to making the US what everyone expects the US to be.

Well written. Not heavy on ego. Not imperious.

Like the book, the thesis—other than the subject matter—was simply not Archie-ish. The pacing, voice, and feel were not the same as the book either. Interesting.

I closed that window, leaving Timothy's thesis, *A Brief Examination of the Richness Dialects Bring to Linguistic Culture*, open on my desktop. It was seventy-five well-written pages of material that I found more interesting than Archie's thesis. And not just the subject matter. It was interesting because 1) it was the same voice as Archie's thesis, but 2) like Archie's thesis, it didn't match the book.

Neither matched the book. Only each other.

Not that I'd really expected them to match the book. I felt vindicated.

The writing was the key.

But it still remained to figure out who had helped write—or totally wrote—the book. And was it the book that mattered the most? Academically, perhaps not. The thesis and dissertation, along with any articles Archie had published in anthropological journals, were the biggies, academically. But there was no denying that the book mattered to his peers as well now that Archie was nationally known.

And what about Archie's and Timothy's dissertations? Would they match both of the theses? Would one match one and not the other, and how to interpret it? That would depend on the match.

And where was I going with all of this?

I hated to admit to myself that I was starting to lose my focus on it all. What was happening with Jebbin, Chatty, Antonia and the world of forensics? Whom did I suspect and whom did I not? And Molly was giddy over Freddy what's-his-name... What *was* his name?

Give it a few moments, I told myself, and it will pop into my head.

The name didn't pop. Everything else was popping around the confines of my skull like popcorn kernels in hot oil bouncing off the walls of the popper.

I needed to think.

I needed space to think.

Out of the house.

It wasn't sunset yet, though the sun was headed that way. I decided to go that way too; west to a broad vista and hopefully a broader perspective on this problem. I stuffed my cell phone into my purse, told the cats to behave themselves, told the dog to come with me as I grabbed the leash off its hook by the door, went into the garage, loaded up Sophie, and drove away in our yellow Beetle.

I felt the freedom I always feel when I hit the road in the car, especially when I was heading out of town into the open countryside. It was a wonderful sensation of being able to go anywhere I wanted, knowing there was this huge network of interconnected roads. Little dirt roads connected with narrow two-lane paved roads that lead to broader state roads that grafted themselves to the interstates. I paused my thoughts a moment to give thanks that I could even have that feeling when I know there are many places in this world where such wanderings are not allowed.

I got onto I-55, then onto I-155 heading north, then off the interstate and left onto US 136, west toward Missouri. I could, if the fit took me, go halfway into Nebraska on this road. but I wasn't planning on going for that long a ramble. I was going ten miles to the Twombly College Observatory on the southern side of Elder Hill, and Highway 136 is the easiest way to get to the road that runs along the Prairie Hills. The observatory opened in 1862, proudly housing a 50-inch Cassegrain-style reflecting telescope, the same style as the famous Hale telescope at the Mount Palomar Observatory in California, only one fourth its size. It was eventually replaced with a larger telescope, but the original is on display in the college museum.

The Twomblys owned all the land in Golden County when the county was first incorporated. Bits have been sold over the years, but much of it is still owned by the family. Prairie Hills and the eastern half of the Red River are in Golden County, and most of that area is a wildlife refuge and nature park, set aside as such in perpetuity by the Twomblys. Only the medium-sized town of Rawlston, at the mid-point north to south of the county, is independent from the Twombly holdings along the river. A bridge there takes Highway 136 across into Schuyler County on its way to Missouri.

I drove through Rawl's Gap, down onto the flood plain on the western side of the ridge, then turned left onto Ridge Road. A few more miles and another left up into the hills on Stargazer Drive soon brought me to the grounds around the observatory. It's as close to "on top of the world" as you can get in Golden County, Illinois.

Sophie and I got out of the car, stopping to retrieve the pillow we keep in a plastic bin in the trunk. I walked her in the dog park until her needs were met, tidied up after her, then let her run while I went to sit on top of my favorite table. The pillow was for sitting on or putting under my head if I decided to lie on my back and look up at the stars. I looked out over the land.

I just breathed for awhile. Looked and breathed.

The sun was maybe half an hour from setting, bright upon the flood plain and the sharp cliffs of the hills on my right while sending the long shadows of the hills across the prairie and farmlands to my left. Ahead of me, the Prairie Hills grew gradually lower until they blended into the plains in the hazy distance.

I hoped Molly was all right. That she was learning, having fun, seeing all sorts of art and architecture she's only read about and seen photos of before. That Freddy what's-his-name was . . . well . . . it seemed pathetic to hope he was a nice boy, despite taking her to a Jack the Ripper Walk and on a tour of the "real" Paris. For one, he was a young man not a boy, and "nice" is so nonspecific. For that matter, I hoped Molly would be a "nice" girl/young woman. I hadn't bargained for a love interest when I agreed to use some of the inheritance money to fund her summer in Europe. If I found out they didn't behave, they'd find me after them with my fencing saber.

Saber!

Sword!

Wilkinson!

Freddy's last name was Wilkinson, like the sword company that ended up making razor blades.

With a smile and a sigh, I mentally crossed one thing off of my "to think about" list. And, all right, I wouldn't actually go after them armed and dangerous, but Jebbin and I would just cross that bridge when we came to it. No sense in trying to decide what we'd do before anything happened … if it ever did.

On to the next item on my agenda.

Murder.

And writers.

A writer, ghost writer, or plagiarizer turned murderer. No, Timothy had been the one rumored to be a plagiarizer and he was now a victim, not the killer. Maybe the murderer was the victim of a plagiarizer? Archie sure seemed to be a massive plagiarizer. I huffed a rueful chuckle as I remembered that the word plagiarism comes from Latin and Greek words meaning to kidnap. Archie had been a life-long kidnapper of other people's thoughts and work.

My thoughts wandered on. What was I doing anyway? I'm no detective. I love reading mysteries, that's true. But really . . . I get wee inklings. Intuition? Hmm. I suppose. That tingle trickling down my spine, that all over sudden quiver. But really . . .

This wasn't a story in a book. This was real. Archie was real. Timothy was real. All the people at the Midwest Anthropological Studies Society's conference were real. Real people were really dead and here I was, some nutcase of a middle-aged homemaker thinking

I could make like a fictional old lady and solve the mystery.

Dear Lord, what was I thinking?

No. No. And no.

Leave it to Jebbin and Chatty. To Jason, Captain Schneider, and Dr. Antonia.

Leave it to the pros.

Woof! Woof, woof!

I nearly slid off the table as Sophie came running my way, barking her head off. I shivered with a chill that had nothing to do with intuition and a lot to do with terror. Why had I come to a park alone at dusk?

Sophie got to the table and kept on going.

Okay. I guess the murderer wasn't right behind me.

My spine tingled but I didn't shiver. It was a pleasant feeling, not a scary one.

Jairus.

The name popped into my head, but I ignored it. I wasn't falling for my "intuition" any more.

"Sophie's not angry." I heard my own voice speaking. "Listen."

Good point, self. She didn't sound like she did when defending her turf.

"How did she look as she ran by?" my inner voice prompted.

Ah . . . Happy. Yes. Like she looked when we were out walking and she'd spot Jebbin coming our way.

"Sophie! How's the good doggy tonight? Huh?" A hearty male voice addressed my dog. "You watching your mama? Are you? Are you keeping a good eye on her? Let's go let her know who's here, if she hasn't figured it out already."

I turned around. His voice confirmed what I already knew.

"Good evening, Jairus. What brings you up here?"

Sophie clambered up onto the seat of the picnic table, grinning, as dogs seem to do much better than cats. "He's okay, Mom. Right?" Her expression, happy eyes, and wagging tail spoke clearly: "We know him. I know him. Did I do good, Mom?" I eased myself off the tabletop, joined her on the bench, and ruffled her ears.

"Yes, you're a good girl Sophie."

"Keep an eye out, Soph," Jairus said as he sat across from us.

Sophie got on top of the table and lay down. From there she could see the entire hilltop area.

I shook my head and chuckled. "You Twomblys. No wonder folks back in old England accused the family of being witches."

My comment didn't shock him. With Jebbin's twenty-three years here at Twombly, we'd already had the 'WOW! Witches, huh?' conversation. He just grinned.

"Is there anything your family doesn't end up knowing ahead of time?"

"There's tons of stuff I don't know, or I wouldn't be so anxious for Jebbin and Dr. Chatterjee to present me with the solution to the murders. We Twomblys are taught to take what the good Lord sends and be patient for the rest. Well . . . as patient as we can. I've never been too successful with the patient part."

"Taught?"

"From father, and sometimes mother as well, to child for more generations than we have record of. And that's a lot, as we have records back to 1154."

I nodded, hoping he could see the gesture in the fast fading light. I didn't quite believe it. For some reason, it just seemed a long way back to have records, for a non-noble family. I started working out in my head how many generations that would be.

"How long has it been in your family?"

"Huh? What?" His question brought my mental calculations to a halt.

"The gift."

"Ah . . ."

"How long has it been in your family?" He tilted his head to give me a quizzical look. "Or don't they talk about it much? I've met others whose families never spoke of it and children were always told to hush or got punished when they'd start to talk about knowing things."

"Um..."

I was being so articulate. I looked across the table at Jairus. The security lights for the observatory had come on. The soft lights barely lit the area, and even then they were always shut off when there was someone using the reflecting telescope. The light glowed on his face, woke hazy glints in his green-gray eyes. There was a gentle look of concern and understanding there.

"I... we... Ah, Jebbin knows. AnnaMay Langstock knows. I think Molly has it but, even with how close we are, she's never said anything and I've not brought it up." I looked over at Sophie, proudly keeping watch. She put her head down for me to scratch behind her ears and I obliged. "Um. My family... my parents that is... never talked about it. Well, not in a good way. My mom didn't talk about very many things in a positive light, but particularly not my dad's family. His mother had it, I know she did, but she never spoke about it, per se. Little hints got dropped here and there, but I'm sure she knew mom wouldn't approve."

I looked back at Jairus. He was watching me intently, but for all the intensity of it, it wasn't threatening. He nodded for me to go on.

"Thing is, my mom had it too. Granny Jeffries was an Appalachian mountain granny, if you know what I mean."

"I do. She was a healer, a midwife, knew all the herb lore and superstitions. She was the one people went to with their troubles and she would often get "a knowin'" about it."

"Yes! That's it exactly." I nodded. Vigorously. "I didn't see her as often as I would have liked to; she was a cheery lady unlike her daughter. She told me I had it. Had the sight, as she called it, and like your people, she gave the credit to the Lord. 'It be a blessin' from the Lord on high. Halleluiah! Praise Jesus!' she'd always say, and Mom would scowl if she was around to hear. And she'd say, 'Ya got it double, Emory-girl. Your Pa's mama, she's got it too. The good Lord done showed me that. Praise His name!' But she had to be careful. She would usually make sure Mom wasn't within hearing distance when she talked about it, and she'd only say a snippet then hush up."

Jairus smiled. "You sound southern when you talk about her."

"Well, with Mom being from the northern Georgia part of the Appalachians and Dad being from the Golden Isles of southern Georgia, that kind of makes me southern."

We both laughed.

"My father was a United Methodist minister and he used it to see some of the country. We spent seven of my growing-up years in Minnesota. That went a long way to knocking the southern out of my accent. But even then, my brother, sister, and I were the only kids in town who said, 'Uff-da, y'all.'"

We laughed some more and then the bubbly feeling subsided.

"You need to embrace your gift, Emory." Jairus's voice was soft and soothing. Enticing. "If you've got a double dose of it, you're doubly blessed, if you choose to see it that way. Use it."

"I . . ."

"You are the one who'll find the answer."

He didn't say what answer.

He didn't need to.

"I don't know what the heck I'm doing, Jairus. I've got it in my fool head that I'm Agatha Christie's Miss Marple. Dear old Jane Marple talking to people in her non-threatening old lady manner, quietly knitting as she figures out who the killer is. But that's foolishness. The only reason I have a bachelors degree is because Jebbin talked the board into mashing all my miscellaneous credit hours together to make one up. I didn't major in anything. I can hardly seem to tie myself down to any one thing, ever. I couldn't even hold a job outside my home. Whatever in the world makes me think . . ."

"You'll figure it out."

That calm, quiet voice pulled me up sharper than a shout ever would have.

"I don't know all you're doing." He reached over to place his hand over mine. His smile added to his tone. "Like I said, I never get shown everything. Always bits of the picture get left out. But I know that whatever it is you're doing, it's the right direction to go. What Jebbin and Dr. Chatterjee, Dr. Conti, and the law enforcement folks are doing will seal the deal. They'll turn out the stuff they'll need in court to make what you find stick. But you're going to figure it out."

"I . . . I'm not sure if I hope you're right or wrong, Jairus. It suddenly feels like a huge responsibility. It doesn't seem to feel like it does when I read about all the sleuths in the mystery books. Like it will make the bright sun shine at the end of a long rainy season. I've the feeling that it won't make things right in the end."

I looked into his eyes.

"Am I making any sense?"

"Yes." He turned to stare into the darkness for a moment, gathering his thoughts I guessed. "Dr. Dawson didn't seem to have had many close friends, just a lot of acquaintances, closer acquaintances, and a wife he wasn't close to. But lives will be changed from his being murdered instead of just passing away. Dr. Law, I've been told, wasn't married, his parents are both gone, no siblings either. But I think he had friends. Real friends. He'll be missed. Lives will be changed because of his murder as well. Whoever did this will carry it with them to the grave, and perhaps beyond. And the people in that person's life will also be changed forever. No. It will bring closure to some, and perhaps even justice, but no; it won't make everything right again."

Sophie got down off the table top and walked toward our cars. Jairus nodded his head toward her.

"Animals have gifts too. I was just going to say it's time to head back to Twombly."

We walked over to the parking lot, beeping our car locks in unison.

"Thank you, Jairus."

"You are most welcome, Emory." His smile was gentle. "Now that you know I know about your gift, call me if you need to talk to someone who understands."

"I will, though I'll tell Jebbin if I do. Don't want it to look unseemly." I chuffed and rolled my eyes. "How's that for an old-fashioned expression? Unseemly. I want it all above board. I'm not interested in messing up my marriage . . . or yours."

"Me neither, believe me. Although Amy isn't very understanding about my giftedness. But, she isn't as vague as she likes to appear. If I tell her you are interested in paranormal things and want to talk to me from time to time about my gift, that'll do. She thinks it's paranormal mumbo-jumbo anyway, but she has her own gift—she can see through a lie a mile or two away. That we were talking about giftedness is the truth. I won't tell her you have it too . . . unless you want me to?"

"No. As the saying goes, the fewer who know, the better."

"I agree. Good night, Emory, and remember what I said tonight."

"I will. Thank you and drive carefully."

"You too." He looked at Sophie. "You're a good dog, Sophie-girl. Keep an eye on your people."

I let Sophie into the back seat, plopped myself in the front, started the car, and drove away with the headlights on. Jairus followed me until we got onto US 136 and were no longer out in the boonies on empty country roads. He flashed the lights on his Mercedes as he passed me. I, on the other hand, drove more slowly than I usually do. My mind wasn't on my driving, which isn't a good way to drive, so I decided to stay in the right lane and go slow.

Jairus told me to remember what he'd said.

He said I'd figure it out.

CHAPTER 15

I was on College Avenue, nearly home, when my purse started playing "Foggy Mountain Breakdown." I dug out my cell phone as I stopped at a stop sign and put the phone on speaker.

"Hi, sweetie!"

"I'm home. Where the hell are you?"

"I'm sorry, Jebbin. I should have called."

"It would have been nice. Where are you?"

"I'm on College Avenue, almost home."

"With all that's going on and you just get in the car and leave without telling anyone? I called the Martins and the Purtles. I called AnnaMay. Nobody knew where you were. Where were you? Never mind, I hear the garage door opening. I'll talk to you when you get in the house."

I pulled into the garage, turned off the car, and sat there a moment. I really hadn't been thinking. I should have called or texted Jebbin. The Martins and Purtles are the neighbors on either side of our house, AnnaMay is my best friend, and I hadn't thought to let any of them know where I was either. Jebbin was right, with all that was happening he had every right to be furious.

I slunk into the house like a dog with its tail between its legs. Sophie did slink in with her tail between her legs.

Jebbin was only a few feet back from the door to the enclosed porch. He took hold of my shoulders, stooping down to look me in the eyes.

"What in the world did you think you were doing?"

"I . . . I . . ."

I felt Sophie hiding behind my legs.

"You weren't thinking. You didn't think about it at all, did you?"

For a moment, other voices from throughout my life joined Jebbin in that scathing phrase. *"You didn't think at all, did you?"* For a moment I shrank, wanting to curl up inside myself like I always had and probably will again, but this time I didn't. Jairus telling me that I was pointed in the right direction emboldened me. I glared right back at my husband.

"Quite the opposite, I was thinking too much. I had so much going round and round in my head that the house felt claustrophobic, and I needed room to think all the thoughts. Room for them to spread out. No. I wasn't thinking about you, other than how overloaded you and Chatty and everyone else is who's working on this. I wasn't thinking, 'Gee, I should call the neighbors and let them know where I'm going.' There wasn't room for that left in my head. In fact, most of the time when I get accused of messing up for 'not thinking,' I've messed up because I have too many thoughts and I can't tie them down or organize them and obvious things get lost in the clutter."

Jebbin's blue eyes were wide with surprise. He pulled me close and hugged me in a tender, tight embrace, like a mother tiger carrying her cub and not breaking its skin with her hunter's teeth.

"I was so scared." His breath made a warm spot as he whispered against the side of my head. "I was picturing Archie and Dr. Law dead in the beautiful gardens and was so afraid that that's where you were. Dead in one of the gardens."

"Oh, Jebbin. I'm so sorry, hon."

We just stood there awhile.

I realized I was still holding my cell phone. I moved my hand to where I could see it and pushed a button to light up the screen.

"I did have my phone with me. The missed calls icon's there. I don't know why it didn't ring through."

My wandering attention went back to what my husband had said while we were hugging.

"Why would I end up in one of the gardens?" I couldn't bring myself to put the word 'dead' in there.

He leaned back in our embrace so he could look at me, shaking his head with a wry grin on his face. "You really don't see, do you? And you need to learn it if you're gonna play at being Miss Marple." He snuggled against me again. "You've been talking to people. Checking books out of the library. Lunching with the lady who ran their registration table. And God knows what else because I sure don't know what else. Someone may have noticed." His arms tightened around me. "Someone who has already killed twice."

"You really think . . . ?" If it was possible to get closer to him, I did. I felt chilled, as though an autumn fog had just rolled in.

"Yeah, I really think what I just said. I've noticed, but . . . well I knew about your sleuthing ambitions from the get-go. Still, even with how busy I've been, I've still been aware of some of what you've been doing. If I'm aware of it, why wouldn't someone who's running scared notice?"

Jebbin took me by the shoulders again. Gently. Warmly. Not with the anger of fear as he had when I first walked in.

"You need to be careful. You need to always have your phone and you need to let me know if you're going somewhere. No matter how safe a place may seem to you, you need to let me know so that someone knows where you are and so I don't panic again."

His grip tightened again.

"Now, for the umpteenth time, where were you?"

I felt more like a naughty child now than when he had used the dreaded "you weren't thinking" phrase, because now I could really see what a dangerous thing I had done. Perhaps that was another reason Jairus Twombly had shown up. Maybe his gift, maybe God, had sent him not just to encourage me, but because his chemistry professor's wife had put herself in danger.

I wished God would have said something to *me* about it.

My mind slipped back to Jebbin's question.

"I went to Observatory Park."

His eyes widened, looked heavenward beseeching help in dealing with his none-too-cautious wife, then closed for a moment of calm. They opened as his eyebrows rose.

"You went, by yourself . . ."

"Wuff," Sophie discreetly interrupted. She was still behind me, tucked up against my legs. I could feel her swaying as she started wagging her tail.

Jebbin looked down at her. "My apologies, Sophie."

He looked back at me. "So you at least had the sense to take Sophie with you." He exhaled and relaxed a little. "That probably wasn't the best way to say that, was it? I'm glad you took Sophie with you. But I really wish you would have called me, or called somebody if you weren't wanting to interrupt my sitting on my butt watching Chatty do all the work."

I put my left hand to my chest since my right had the phone in it and drew a cross over my heart. "I will call from now on, always. Cross my heart and hope . . ." I sucked in the next two words. They weren't right for this situation. I held up my pinky finger. "Pinky swear?"

Jebbin smiled as he looped his bigger pinky finger around mine.

"Pinky swear works for me. And I promise the same. If I go somewhere unexpected, I'll call or text you."

I broke our link first, turning toward the fridge.

"Are you hun . . . Wait a minute. Why are you home? Didn't I ask you to not come home for dinner?" I felt my face heat up. "Ah, I mean . . ."

"Yeah, exactly." He looked as I imagine he would look at a

student who thought they'd gotten away with cheating then put their foot in it. "'Oh, Jebbin,'" he mimicked me, "'I just don't feel up to fussing with dinner. I think I'll take a nice warm shower and go to bed early.' I'll admit, you were convincing. I never reckoned you were planning to escape."

"Well, at first I wasn't. I had something else I had to do, but now you're the one avoiding a direct question. Why are you home?"

He pulled out a chair from the small kitchen table and turned it around to sit with his forearms resting on the back. "You just go ahead with taking care of that 'are you hungry' question you started to ask because yes, I am, and I'm sure you are too. I came home because I have something I thought my apprentice, Miss Marple, would want to know."

"Ok. Hmm. There isn't much here. We've been doing carry out lately."

I opened the freezer and shoved things around looking for something to heat up for us.

"Chili? I've definitely got enough for a bowl each, and . . . Ah . . . Yes! I have cornbread muffins too. That sound good to you?"

"Wonderful."

"Great. I'll reheat whilst you spill the beans."

"I thought the beans were in the chili."

I turned to see a devilish grin on his face.

"Very good, Dr. Crawford. Now, tell me your news or I won't start nuking the food."

"Yes 'm." He saluted me, I turned back to the freezer to take out our dinner, and he started talking.

"Well, Dr. Timothy Law didn't just lay himself down and let the killer put that board and those rocks on him. Like Archie before him, he was drugged into submission first."

"That makes sense." I put the muffins into the microwave to thaw them a little before finishing them up in the toaster oven. I'd nuke the chili while the muffins were heating through.

"Yep. Indeed it does. What makes even more sense is that it was another herbal poison. Aconitum uncinatum, otherwise known as North American monkshood."

"Ewww! That's nasty stuff."

The microwave beeped. I opened the door, took the muffins out, and put the chili in. Punched buttons to get it going again, then popped the muffins into the toaster oven. I was just about to turn it on when I remembered it had gone berserk and been unplugged. I took the muffins out. We'd get along with crumbling them up and pouring the chili over them.

"If I remember correctly," I said while working, "it is even poisonous to the touch."

"Right. The poison can get you any way you look at it. Since the aconite alkaloids can be absorbed through the skin, you don't even have to get your victim to swallow it. From what Antonia found out and then what we confirmed, Dr. Law didn't have a chance. One of Antonia's assistants was touching Law's hands, you know, looking for any clues—skin under the nails and that sort of thing. A short while later, he mentioned that one of his fingers felt tingly and he noticed a tear in his glove. Antonia immediately thought "poison" and hustled the student to the sink, where she pulled his gloves off and put them in an evidence bag, turned the water on and squirted soap onto his hands, then sent him to the ER on the first floor of the hospital. She quickly did some checking of Law's body and found evidence in his throat that he'd vomited. His mouth and face had been cleaned up, but the killer couldn't wash out his throat. She immediately took samples and sent them to her lab and to Chatty and me. Everything came back to indicate aconite poisoning, without a doubt."

I was getting out bowls and plates even though eating was becoming less appealing by the second.

"So, ingested and tactile?"

"Yep. Not sure of the delivery method for the skin absorption, but we know the ingestion was Earl Grey tea. There were enough traces in his throat and stomach. The monkshood causes tingling, like Antonia's assistant felt, and numbness pretty quickly. It doesn't always cause the vomiting, but with Timothy getting it via both absorption and ingestion, I'm sure it hit him rather strongly and fast. Lethal dose is around five milligrams, and Antonia figures he had nearly double that. He would have been having trouble breathing, been uncoordinated, and experiencing whatever else having severe low blood pressure and a host of cardio-pulmonary issues would cause. It wouldn't have taken long at all before he couldn't defend himself, and his heart rate and breathing would have been so badly affected that it didn't need much weight to do him in."

The microwave announced it was done. I needed to stir the partially thawed chili and run it again.

Instead, I just stared at it.

"Not really great pre-dinner conversation," I said to the microwave's door.

Jebbin came over and hugged me from behind.

"Sorry, hon. You, ah, want to let this sit and we'll eat a while later?"

I breathed slowly . . . In . . . Out. Checked out how I was feeling.

"No. Better eat now. I feel a headache hovering and it will take up residence if I don't eat." I stirred the now unappealing chili and got it nuking again without leaving his embrace. "But I sure don't want any tea with dinner tonight."

I picked up a still cool and firm muffin and worked the paper off of it.

He chuckled and gave me a squeeze. "Me neither," he said as he gave me another squeeze and a peck on my cheek to signal the hug was over. He turned his chair around the "right" way at the table. I finished tearing up the muffins and dishing up, brought everything over to the table, and we ate in the silence of people busy with their own thoughts.

I didn't taste a bit of that meal. I was going to have to spend part of tomorrow arranging all the thoughts in my head—tonight they just weren't going to hold still long enough to tell me anything.

Jebbin and I went to bed early. We cuddled, talking about our kids and our pets and some bluegrass songs we wanted to work on together.

Everything except murder.

CHAPTER 16

Wednesday dawned.

Just as day always does, no matter who has been born or who has "slipped the surly bonds of earth," to borrow a line from the poem "High Flight." The author did not use the phrase as a metaphor for death, but it seemed to fit this morning.

Sometimes, life is surly.

Jebbin was already gone, but I'd expected that.

No.

Change that.

I was good with it. Yesterday had been like riding the Screamin' Eagle at Six Flags in St. Louis. That old-style, wooden roller-coaster that is eleven stories tall on the highest hill sends you zipping around at sixty-two miles per hour. I love roller-coasters, but I prefer them to stay at the amusement park and not become the flow of my life. Now I needed to take all those twists and turns, highs and lows, and make sense out of them. I rolled onto my back to watch the patterns of leaf shadows on the ceiling. Sophie hopped onto Jebbin's side of the bed. Kumquat parked herself between my calves and Hortense lay down on my chest, which would last only until she got too heavy, then I'd move her off to one side on the bed. They always seem to know when I'm in bed having a think.

Highs.

Apparently, I'm on the right track if Jairus' intuition stood up to the bright light of reality shining through my bedroom window. Often such things make perfect sense as night dims the sky and the magic of the stars appears, but seem silly when the light throws everything into sharper contrast. I know the Twombly family is different. I know Jairus is creepy-right most of the time. But I also know neither he nor his ancestors were 100 percent spot on. They had not seen the way clearly many a time. I huffed a chuckle as Amy Twombly's face came into focus on my mind's screen.

But . . .

I deleted Amy from my thoughts. She wasn't a part of this situation.

They were right—Jairus was right—much more than half the time.

That means there's something about the book that's the root of all this evil.

Another high: I liked the idea of Sonya Dawson and Naomi Malkoff becoming friends. There was a sense of cosmic balance to it somehow; to Sonya finding comfort and companionship from someone whom Archie had planned on turning into another crack in their marriage's foundation. My intuition was telling me Naomi needed Sonya too.

Lows.

I'd upset Jebbin last night when he had no energy for it. I'd frightened him by slipping off to have my think. We'd settled it all out, but it was a huge low point.

I was out of murderers.

Technically, I had a whole conference full of potential suspects, just none that seemed to stand out. But then, how could they when I didn't know any of them except:

Dr. Archibald Finlay Dawson—victim. If he hadn't been the first victim, I would have had trouble seeing Archie as a killer anyway. He'd buy someone off long before he'd kill them. If he did pursue something of a permanent nature, I'm sure he'd pay to have the dirty work done by a pro.

Dr. Timothy Law—my prime suspect turned victim. I could have . . . Scratch that, *did* see him as a potential killer, one of those "still waters run deep" sorts. But obviously I'd been wrong.

For a moment, I was swept back into Masaki's garden. Back to Sophie whimpering beside a piece of plywood with some landscaping rocks piled on it. Rippled sand with her paw prints going against the grain. Murders go against the grain of what life should be like.

I couldn't lie there any longer. I worked my right leg out from around Kumquat, and once it was out, she hopped off the bed anyway—typical cat maneuver. Hortense was already out of my way because I'd moved her off my chest to my right side. She merely squinted up at me and put her head back on her paws. Sophie got down as soon as I moved my leg. Unlike the cats who get to take care of life's necessities in the house in a litter box, Soph was more than ready to be let out. I slipped my feet into my Isotoner ballet-style slippers, let happy Sophie out into our backyard, then went to take care of my needs. While in the bathroom, I returned to my thinking.

Myra Fordyce had never struck me as a suspect. I couldn't see her being suckered in by dear Archibald Finlay Dawson. That lady was grounded and independent. Nearly as self-sufficient as her Hutterite friends. But I still had to deal with the thought that you never know. Some of history's worst criminals were charming, intelligent people.

Dr. Cameron Garrow—the displaced 1960s or '70s Mother Earth News cover girl. She would have known the superstitions. I knew that she drank herbal tea, but so do I, and that didn't make me an expert in herbal poisons. I felt she truly was just another person who only knew Archie from the yearly MASS conferences.

Dr. Charles A. Lindberg—ah . . . No. I could definitely see the man hating Archie, the way Archie teased him, but he really seemed to be just another conference acquaintance with insufficient motive to murder his once-a-year tormenter.

Sonya Dawson—hmm . . . Still a possibility I reckon. She was intelligent enough to write that book, but their relationship was not one where I could see her doing anything like that *with* or *for* her husband. A faked paper for school while they were both still students—yes. At this point in their relationship—no. I could see her, with her warm, rich voice, telling her husband to stick the idea of her writing anything for him where the sun don't shine.

Naomi Malkoff might have been a real possibility, except she had just become connected with Professor Dawson this past semester. NOT enough time to write that long, well-researched book.

And that was it. I was done with my ablutions and done with my long, long list of possible suspects. Humph. That brought me into the kitchen to let Sophie in, feed the critters their breakfast, and up against the same wall of "What the heck do you think you're doing, Emory Crawford, playing at being Miss Marple?" Despite Jairus' comments, I was still battling a feeling of behaving like a fool.

I gave my head a shake. Old habits die hard and I'd do my best to send them packing. Eventually. For now, sending them to another corner of my mental room would be a worthy start. I made my own breakfast, suffering with my usual view of myself as a failure cowering in a corner with the dust bunnies. With my meal on a tray, I started for the deck and decided to take something to read with me.

If Archie's book could have jumped up and hollered, it couldn't have got my attention any better. Its siren song of murder drew my eyes toward it. What had I just been thinking? My list of suspects. Naomi. Naomi not having time to write such a well-researched book. Well-researched. I was only assuming it was well-researched from the main content; I hadn't touched the appendices at the end. Appendices are where research shines its brightest. *The Devil's Music* got added to my tray and the two of us, along with the cats and dog, settled down at, on, and beside the table.

I took my multivitamin, my blood pressure pill, and my antidepressant, then dove into both my meal and the book. There were two appendices: "Song Stories Not Covered in the Text" and "Superstition vs. Faith in Early American Folk Music"—the usual sorts of things that some readers might like to know but that don't fit well into the body of the book.

"Song Stories" filled in details about several songs mentioned in the text that had been written about real life murders. For example, "Poor Ellen Smith," the song by an unknown author, was based on the 1894 murder of Ellen Smith in Winston-Salem, North Carolina. Ellen was a love-struck girl whom the town drunk had made use of, only to break up with her when she became pregnant. The baby died soon after being born, and Ellen began stalking her former lover, Peter DeGraff. He eventually sent her a note that was worded to sound like he wanted to be with her again, asking her to meet him in the woods. When she showed up, he shot her in the chest. He confessed to the crime from the gallows just before he was hung. The song was written at the time and has been sung ever since.

I read the appendix more thoroughly than I'd intended to. Between reading and thinking (Daydreaming? Yes, some of that too), I ended up sitting there nearly two hours. I got up, toted the tray into the kitchen, loaded dirty dishes into the washer, set Archie's book on the counter, hung up the tray, and then decided to take Sophie for a short walk to work the kinks out of both of us. I walked to the porch door where her leash hung and stopped in mid-reach. My hand stayed poised a second or two before slowly dropping.

No.

No doggy romps on the campus until all this was over and done with and the murderer in custody. I wanted no temptations to wander into any of Twombly College's gardens.

I went to scoop dog piles out of our backyard instead; a good, earthy, back to nature sort of thing that requires little to no thinking.

I clipped dead lilac heads off the large bush in the back west-side corner of the yard and checked out the buds forming on my Mr. Lincoln, Tropicana, and Radiant Perfume roses. Anything to avoid going back to "work."

I finally realized it must be getting near lunch time, and barely got the deli-chicken sandwiches made before Jebbin and Chatty rushed in.

"Tomorrow's the last full day of the conference," Jebbin said between huge, hasty bites.

"Mm." Chatty nodded, swallowed, and continued. "Yes, yes. And we have not turned up that most vital clue that will tell us who done it, as the saying goes."

"Jason said the police are looking closer at a few of the women conferees. Apparently, word has slowly come out that they've had relationships of one sort or the other with Archie or Timothy." Jebbin drank down half his glass of lemonade while Chatty filled in more information.

"Indeed. As well as ones that have been observed drinking herbal teas at meals." His exaggerated upward glance was all the more pronounced because of his dark brown eyes and dark caramel skin. "As though that really matters. Many, many people drink such teas yet know nothing about any other herbs."

"That's true," I put in while both men had their mouths full. "It really doesn't seem to be a sufficient reason to suspect someone."

Jebbin stood, grabbed his empty plate and glass, kissed me on the head as he crossed to the trash, and said, "Done and gone," before planting a peck on my cheek and heading for the front door. Chatty balanced his plate and glass in one hand.

"I have not finished. I'll bring the plate and glass back at dinnertime. Wait for me, Jebbin!"

They were out before I could even swallow my bite of sandwich to say goodbye.

I felt a tug at the back of my mind. I turned to look at The Book sitting on the counter. If it had legs and feet it would have been standing there tapping its foot in an irritated rhythm. I glared at it.

"Yeah, yeah, yeah. You're as pushy as Archie was, even though I'm certain he didn't write any of you."

I tidied up after myself, picked up Archie's, or whoever's, book, got comfy on my chaise, and started the other appendix.

"Superstition vs. Faith" would be interesting I felt, although I already knew a fair amount about those subjects and how they interrelated. There had been a strong mix of both in the times of the Middle Ages and the eras that followed. There were people who, while strongly into the "old ways," sprinkled them with a bit of Christianity, and the opposite was also true. Even the most ardent Christian still believed many of the superstitions and supernatural stories that had been the tenets of the pre-Christian religions. It all seemed too strange to me. Then, I paused. It shouldn't seem strange. A lot of Christians I knew would knock on wood, were careful about Friday the thirteenth, and didn't like black cats.

"Merowwwooo."

I looked over the top of the book toward the end of the chaise. Hortense was glaring at

me. No . . . At the book was more precise.

"Meroww."

How did she know what I'd been thinking about people and black cats?

"It's alright, my dear Hortense." I rubbed her cheek with my big toe, and she closed her eyes to lean into the rub. "Those silly people had no idea how wrong they were. And don't forget, in England and Japan black cats are lucky."

"Mumph!" she huffed, as though to say at least someone had it right, then put her head back down on her paws.

Cats.

I shook my head and got back on my train of thought. Yes, I even personally knew a lady who considered herself to be a Christian astrologer. Her office walls where she saw clients were covered with astrology symbols and charts, crosses, and pictures of Jesus.

Ah well, back to the book. The author—I really couldn't call it Archie's book any longer — began by saying that since the title referred to "the devil's music," he or she felt that the subject of superstition versus Christian faith should be addressed. I was sucked in deeper as the first item to be discussed was the Salem Witch Trials.

> "In that era, it was easy for the citizens of Salem to recognize signs of the devil and his work because all the superstitions were still an active part of their culture. They would know the things that were bad omens and those that were good. They would recognize objects that indicated a curse had been placed upon their person, their family, their possessions, or their property."

I hadn't really thought about that, but it was a valid point to make. The sixteen hundreds were as steeped in superstition as the Middle Ages had been. "Doctors" were still the people who knew the old ways with herbs and words that were said over their patients. Warts were removed by rubbing them with a small piece of raw meat, then the meat was to be buried and you were to visualize the meat as being your wart, and as it rotted and broke down, so would your wart. Then there was moonshine and poke root aged together. The elixir was taken, one tablespoon a day, to ease the pain and swelling of arthritis.

I know a lot of this sort of weird stuff because both my grandmas knew the old ways and, to varying degrees, clung to them.

I read more about the Salem trials, though I didn't find myself as transported as I had been when I'd done my research before. At that time, I'd felt as if I was there. Then, when I was nearly to the 'I'll just skim over this' stage, a phrase loomed bold on the page.

> "Elizabeth Proctor was not hung, as was her husband. Nothing is said to indicate it, but this author wonders if she did 'plead the belly' to put off her execution. The phrase

refers to a rather long-held British law allowing women who were sentenced to death but claimed to be pregnant the chance to stave off being hung for their crime until after their child was born. It was not perceived as murder to execute a criminal, but it was seen as murder to kill an unborn child, and the Crown didn't want to be viewed as a murderer. This 'escape clause' was often abused, as female prisoners could go several months without it seeming strange that they were not showing an enlarged belly. However, it was surprising how often cases turned around during that time and the woman was set free before the evidence of her claim presented itself. In Elizabeth Proctor's case, she truly was expecting, and she gave birth to her son, who she named John after his executed father, on January 27, 1693."

"Plead the belly. Plead the belly." I looked down the length of my legs at Hortense. She deigned to raise her head and open her eyes in response. "I've heard that. When? When did I hear that?"

I tried to shut off some of my wayward thoughts so I could more clearly hear the voice saying that strange phrase. If I could hear the voice, then I'd most likely see where I was when I had heard it.

Hortense stood, stretched front and back, then glided up the seat of the chaise until she could bump her head against my hand. I stroked the top of her head and cheekbones.

"There were lots of people around. Eating. Hmm... Sunday Brunch! It was the Sunday Brunch for the MASS Conferees. Tell Mommy she's doing well, Hortense."

I lifted her chin so she looked at me.

"Mrrrr," she said, blurring a meow and purr.

I chose to take that as an affirmative response.

"Thank you. Now who was it? I don't really... No, it isn't a man's voice, so it couldn't have been Timothy. Myra?" I tried to think of what we had talked about. But Myra didn't materialize in my mental version of the school cafeteria.

"No! She wasn't there! Or, at least I didn't talk to her or see her."

My exclamation startled Hortense, who scooted off toward the bedrooms. I shifted my attention to Kumquat who had taken up residency on the table beside the chaise.

"It was Saturday that I talked with Myra over breakfast. Sunday it was Timothy and…"

I closed my eyes and let myself sink into the mushy back of my chair. Yes. Jebbin had barely been there that morning. Swallowed his food whole and left. Then I saw Timothy Law going through the buffet line, he saw me at the table, and I waved him over. We talked about Archie and Sonya.

"He withdrew somewhat when we started talking about Sonya," I told Kumquat without opening my eyes. "That makes all the sense in the world now that I know they were together. Very together. He said . . . Oh my!" My eyes opened but I looked at the ceiling as though it was a cinema screen showing the scene in the dining room with everyone coming and going on cue. Hitting their marks and saying their lines. "He said he thought he knew who did it, just before he got up and left. Just before he left and Cameron cleared her throat and startled me. What do you think, Kumquat? How long was she standing nearby? Close enough to hear what Timothy said? Not so near that he noticed her, I wouldn't think . . ."

Now I could see it all clearly; Dr. Cameron Garrow garbed, as always, like a displaced hippie, looking around her as though she was telling a juicy secret, leaning across the table toward me, her melodious voice saying:

"I've read that spouses are always the first person the police look at in murder cases. If she has been with Timothy, maybe she'll plead the belly if they do accuse her of the murder."

CHAPTER 17

I was out the door without even thinking much about leaving the house, barely remembering to grab my key ring and lock the door. I needed to obtain one more dissertation—Dr. Cameron Garrow's.

Focused on Blythe Hall and the library on the second floor, I crossed the street without looking and barreled along the sidewalk until I ran into Amy Twombly.

Literally.

I had come abreast of a lilac bush on the right side of the sidewalk and out she popped, like some fashionista flasher. She ended up supine in the middle of the sidewalk with me sprawled on top.

"Get off me, you cow!"

I would have loved to have pushed up off her hard, with my knee digging into one of her thigh muscles, one of my pointy, boney elbows stabbing her shoulder... or some other part of female anatomy on the front of the upper torso. My knees and elbows have remained boney and pointy whilst the rest of me has filled out, to put it nicely. Instead, I rolled off to one side.

"Moo," I intoned. "I think it would have been more comfortable to land on the cement rather than all your pokey bones. I do hope you didn't hit your head."

Amy bothered with no further niceties as she gracefully gained her feet, even with four-inch stilettos on, and stood glowering down at me. I gained my feet with all the grace of a walrus out of water, wanting nothing more than to be on my way to AnnaMay and her ability to order people's dissertations.

"What did you do with Jairus?"

I stared blankly at her. Jairus? Had I done something with Jairus? What would I do with Jairus? "I didn't do anything with Jairus."

"Oh, come on. You leave town in that cute little car of yours. He leaves in his stodgy Mercedes not long after and you were both heading toward I-155. So, it shouldn't be too hard a question even for you. What were you doing with my husband?"

"Oh!" I smiled with relief. "Last night, you mean?"

She just glared at me. I really should have expected something like this from her.

"I went to Elder Hill, to the observatory, to think and watch the stars come out. I took our dog, Sophie, with me. Jairus just showed up like he often does. You know, his Twombly Touch. All we did was sit and talk about that, about his gift."

Amy looked frustrated and relieved all at the same time. "Good Lord, not that again. I won't let him talk about that idiotic junk with me. Ooo! The Twomblys have a 'gift.'" She made air-quotes with her well-manicured fingers. "'I just know we need to go to this-and-such place, Amy. I just know I need to talk to so-and-so or whosy-whatsy, Amy.'" She singsonged all this with an empty-headed look on her face. "What a bunch of mush. But what does he and his stupid gift have to do with you, that he'd drive all the way out there to talk to you?"

For a pleasant change my brain didn't go blank. "He was afraid I might have been spooked by his gift, because he had showed up at the murder sites before we'd even called the police or anyone else for that matter."

Amy was silent for several seconds, then raised her hand to tap me on the chest with one long glittery fingernail. "Lucky for you and your dorky chemistry teacher husband that that sounds exactly like something Jairus would do. God help me, he's always so concerned about other people. If the rest of his twerpy family were like that, it's amazing they got so rich. Looking out for number one is the only way to get anywhere in this world."

She quit tapping her finger and her face went blank for a moment. "I lost track of . . . Oh, yeah. Just you remember, Emery Board," the fingernail was stabbing me again, "my husband may think he knows what's going on all the time, but his gift ain't no match for *my* connections. I know what's what, too, so you just steer clear of him or I'll know about it."

She stalked off, her stiletto heels rapping loud and sharp enough to crack the concrete. My feet hurt just listening to it.

"'You just steer clear of him or I'll know about it.'" I mimicked behind her retreating back and sashaying keister. "Careful there, Amy darlin'," I added, my Georgia heritage softening the edges of the words, "or you'll sling your behind right off."

With a dismissive flick of my hand, I waved her off, then turned and hurried on to the library.

"What do you think, AnnaMay?" I leaned over her desk, trying not to pant in her face from my hurry.

"Well . . . it is an odd enough phrase that, yes, I think it's good cause to consider her the possible ghostwriter and send for her dissertation. What do you know about her?"

I leaned back to think. "I, ah. Um. I really don't know much. I don't even remember which school she teaches at. The only thing I remember is that she specialized in pre- through post- Revolutionary War era culture in the northern colonies. I've no idea of how "pre" pre was, or how "post" post was, but that's what she said she studied. She looks like a 1970s back to nature, Mother Earth News sort. Always wears long jumper-style dresses and Birkenstocks. And she didn't like Archie, I know that too. She said something snotty about him when I first met her. Ah. Myra Fordyce said something derogatory about Archie just after he'd rounded the corner into the main entrance foyer on his way out of the Hall, under her breath, mind you. Most anyone who's been in a school building most of their lives knows how sounds carry in a hall when it isn't full of students. I wasn't looking over at the registration table, so I had quite a start when this other voice, very near to my table, said something about him being a jerk. Not quite that but something along those lines. I hadn't heard her approach because of her Birkenstocks."

"Hmm." AnnaMay had her elbows on her desk, hands folded as if she was praying, with her chin resting on her thumbs and the tips of her index fingers just grazing the underside of her nose. One of her favorite thinking poses. "Any idea why she didn't like him? Did she go to school with him like Dr. Law had?"

"No. She's too young to have gone to school with them. They're more our age, mid-forties, and she's early to mid-thirties. I think she said she only knew Archie through the annual MASS conferences. Something about she rarely missed one and had often watched him from afar. Studied him and hadn't liked what she'd observed. She said anthropologists have a tendency to do that: occupational hazard."

"I can believe that." AnnaMay moved her hands away from her face and smiled. "Like I always notice if people have a book with them in restaurants or if they have bookshelves in their homes, and of course, if they do have bookshelves or a book with them, I have to try to see the titles. So, that's all the relationship she claimed?"

"Yep. That was it."

"Not much then, other than her use of that archaic phrase."

"No." I sighed and let my eyes trail off to the left to stare at AnnaMay's "In" and "Out" boxes.

She clicked away on her keyboard while my mind played with the idea of in and out boxes. I should have a set, I thought. My ins and outs were usually jumbled together in various piles on the dining table or my desk in my office/craft room. If I had them, would I even use them? Should I buy a set for both the desk and the table?

"Do they really help you, AnnaMay?"

The clicking hesitated then continued. The head librarian could type and talk at the same time, something I found hard to do.

"You've jumped the track again, Emory. Do what really help me?"

My face warmed a bit. "Sorry. I'm staring at your in and out boxes and wondering if getting some would help me with sorting some of my mes . . . paperwork."

"Mess was more accurate." She quit typing and grinned at me. "You'd have to actually put the incoming papers in the in box and the ones that need to go out in the out box and file the rest in their appropriate places for them to work."

"Hmm." I nodded sagely. "Probably not then."

We both laughed.

AnnaMay looked back at her monitor. "Dr. Cameron Garrow teaches at Maize State Community College in West Des Moines, Iowa, and a request for her dissertation is on its merry way." She looked back at me. "I'll let you know when it gets here."

"Your subtle way of telling me to get out of your hair?"

"Yes. You've been staring at my in and out boxes. I'm swamped today. And anyway, you're a library volunteer so I'm your boss. Out, Emory Crawford."

I returned her wink. "Oh yes, boss lady. I'm on my way, boss lady. I wouldn't dream of taking up too much of your time, boss lady." I paused. "Should I go now?"

She grabbed a book as if to throw it at me, and I left with the sound of our laughter following me through the door.

CHAPTER 18

I was putting the casserole dish of Six-Layer Dinner on the table when Jebbin and Chatty rushed in as though the house was aflame and they were the fire department. As they sat, Jebbin lunged for the serving spoon and hot pad to dig into dinner.

"No!"

He stopped just short of yanking the lid off the glass dish.

I stared both men down. "I'm not going through another meal like lunch. If you don't have time to eat the dinner I've fixed at a reasonable pace, I'd rather dish it up for you in to-go containers and have you take it back to the lab."

Chatty gently shook out his paper napkin before tucking it into his shirt collar, then he sat with his hands folded, resting on the edge of the table.

"I told you, did I not my friend, that we were not gentlemen at lunch? And I was right. There is nothing pressing currently happening at the laboratory. Machines are competently running their various tests and they do so whether we are there watching the lights on them flicker or whether we are not. The only thing pressing is time itself and our taking a bit more of time to enjoy this . . ."

He peered at the transparent brown casserole dish.

"To enjoy this most excellent dish that Emory has set before us will not make a great difference at this point."

Jebbin blushed, grinned, sat back with the spoon and hot pad still in his hands and sighed. "I concede, Dr. Chatterjee, and my apologies, hon. If Lanthan or Molly had acted like I just did when they were kids, they'd have been sent to their rooms with no supper. Pass me your plate, Chatty, and I'll dish up for you."

"Thank you." I smiled as I took my seat at the middle of the long side of the table. "Jebbin, pass his plate this way and I'll put a roll and some salad on it."

When we were all served and eating rather than stuffing the food down, I asked the guys how things were going.

"Well," Jebbin began, "Jason stopped in and said they had checked the tea and herbal medicine stashes of everyone known to bring their own teas with them to meals or who had a reputation for using herbal meds. Said if we, or Antonia's lab, don't find poisons among that bunch, they'll get an expanded warrant to search everyone's rooms."

Chatty tugged a piece of paper from his shirt pocket then held it out to me. "I wrote down the names of those already searched for you, Emory, as I was not sure I would remember them all. Everything was taken by the police and we have been testing samples from these all afternoon."

I looked at the list. There were several names on it I didn't recognize, but a few belonged to people I had come to know.

Sonya Dawson—staying at the Victorian Lady B&B—known to use Greek herbal medicines. Had a small zip bag of herbs for indigestion and one for headaches. She also had a small jar of homemade herbal face cleanser and a small jar of homemade herbal face cream.

Myra Fordyce—in small, handmade wooden boxes with handwritten labels—had herb blends for arthritis, indigestion, headaches, high blood pressure, and one to relieve sinus congestion. She also had small jars of homemade herbal face cleanser, face cream, and hand cream and several small tins of homemade tea mixtures, as well as several commercial packets of regular teas—Bigelow brand—including Earl Grey.

Dr. Cameron Garrow had a small carry bag full of a large variety of herbal medicines in crushed leaf, powder, and liquid forms as well as several custom blend herbal teas in zip bags and in "Stash" tea company tins. Included was a box of Twining's brand Earl Grey.

My other familiar person, Naomi Malkoff, wasn't on the list and must not be a tea drinker or into herbal medicines. Of course, at this point Cameron was of particular interest to me, and she did have Earl Grey tea with her.

I thought about telling the guys about my current line of inquiry—gosh that sounded so official—but decided not to. I'd headed off in the wrong direction once already and didn't really want to make some grandiose, final chapter of a mystery book pronouncement that I now knew who'd done it. No. I'd wait till I checked out Cam's dissertation.

Waiting.

We all spend a fair amount of our time waiting. Waiting for our birthday or Christmas when we're kids. Waiting for the school bus. Waiting in various lines in all the various places we go as adults. Waiting in traffic. Waiting for the bad news—or the good news.

With all the practice we get at waiting, we rarely seem to accept it gracefully. Few people like to wait. Sometimes I don't mind. I view it as a chance to pull out a book to read or pull out some portable handcraft I'm working on.

Tonight, I was minding the wait.

There was no chance of getting Cameron's dissertation tonight, so the evening dragged by. I watched TV and knitted. No. I had the TV on, but I wasn't watching it; I barely listened to it. And when I did pay attention to the knitting, it was only to find I'd made silly mistakes in the simple knit four, purl four checkerboard pattern.

I was too busy waiting . . .

. . . and wondering . . .

. . . and worrying.

Was I wrong again? Would Dr. Cameron Garrow end up like my first suspect, Dr. Timothy Law? Was I somehow jinxing these people? I shook my head sharply to dislodge that thought. It wasn't right and it wasn't in the least productive. But then again, nothing I was thinking was productive.

Not producing, just waiting.

Finally, about midnight, I hauled myself off to bed to see what dreams might come.

CHAPTER 19

The dreams came: more weird ones.

Timothy and Archie were following me around. They'd appear around the end of the library stack shelves and just stare at me. They sat at my kitchen table. They went with me while I walked Sophie. Then, they went away, and Cameron, Myra, Sonya, Naomi, AnnaMay, and Aine McAllister followed me around like a female Greek chorus in a play, telling some invisible audience what I was thinking and feeling and how it was all a result of my past.

I woke up thinking I preferred the guys' ghostly presences. At least they were quiet.

AnnaMay's call came at nine forty-two. Don't you just love digital clocks for that usually needless exactness?

"It has arrived."

"What, I don't even get a hello? What if Jebbin had answered?"

"He's in his beloved laboratory blissfully unaware of our behind-the-scenes collusion."

I sighed in her ear. "We aren't being deceitful; after all, it isn't illegal for you to ask for dissertations."

"No, but the secretive part suits nicely and, anyway, collusion is a word I've always liked the sound of." AnnaMay huffed a chuckle. "When are you coming for it? Or perhaps I should ask why you aren't already here?"

My response was to head out my front door without ending the call. I made it to the last step of the porch before she caught on and I heard her laughing over the open connection before she hung up.

I should have taken time to put on a light sweater. It was one of those early summer, cool, grey days that have such a different feel to them from cool grey autumn days or ones that come in the winter. There's a feeling of remembered warmth from the day before and anticipated warmth in days to come that makes the overcast sky seem sadder than in other seasons.

AnnaMay sat at her desk. Just sat there. She never just sat, she was always reading files, typing away on her computer, or standing at a cabinet, keeping her world in order.

She looked like the cat that just ate Mom's favorite canary.

I knew what that meant.

"You already had a look at it, didn't you?"

"'The Ways of Folks in Early Seventeen Hundreds New England' is interesting for a dissertation."

"You stole my moment." I deflated into her visitors' chair.

AnnaMay's eyes sparkled. "I did find the reverse use of 'folkways' in the title intriguing, and didn't really, I only read the table of contents."

My jaw flopped open. "You . . . you . . ."

I saw that her hands were resting on the dissertation. Faster than an oak-leaf rattler, I snatched the document from under her.

"You horrid tease! It's mine now and you'll never get your evil hands on it again. Never, I tell you. Never!"

I flung my nonexistent cape around me and strode to the door, where I stopped and turned back.

"You'll pay for this somehow, Langstock. Probably by having to put up with my taking you out to dinner somewhere moderately expensive. Thanks for the help getting all the dissertations and theses."

"Any time, Crawford." She winked at me."Longhorn Steakhouse

in Springfield for a medium-rare Flo's Filet & Lobster, the lobster dipped in clarified butter, with a Chocolate Stampede oozing chocolaty goodness for dessert sounds good."

I saw her swallow and figured she was trying not to drool. I knew I was—trying not to, that is, not actually drooling.

"When all this is settled and over, it will be my pleasure. Later, hon."

"Later."

Then I was gone.

Jebbin and Chatty called at twelve thirty, as I was mashing up the egg salad for our sandwiches, to say they were ordering Jimmy John's in at the lab for lunch.

"We just haven't got what we need."

I could hear the exhaustion and frustration in my husband's voice. His side of the bed had shown that he'd been there with me at some point in the night, but I had neither heard him come nor heard him go. I put the phone on speaker and started making my lone sandwich. The rest of the egg salad would get put in the fridge.

"Are you gonna tell Captain Schneider? Going to have them do the more complete search for the poisons?"

"Already did and he wasn't too thrilled. He didn't like the other news—that you and I have been requested to attend the closing dinner of the MASS Conference tonight and perform at it as well. I think the only thing that kept him from tearing my head off was that it was both Dr. Lindberg and Jairus who were basically insisting that we do it."

"And you heard about this, when?"

He hesitated. "I'm sorry, hon. Jairus and Dr. Lindberg came in about ten this morning with the request. Chatty and I were going over everything we've done, feeling under all this pressure to solve the case before everyone goes home—mostly tomorrow morning, but a few are going tonight after the dinner—and I forgot to call you."

"No problem, sweetie. I just hope they don't want murder songs. They don't, do they?"

"No, gonna-miss-you-then-meet-you-over-yonder sorts of songs."

I smiled with relief. "OK, I'll go over some we know well and do up a playlist. Any idea how many?"

"Ah. Hmm. Four. Make it four."

"Ok. See you later when you come home to get ready."

"Yeah, see you then."

Sophie sat at my feet looking up at me, "Why didn't you tell him?" shining in her eyes.

"I'll tell him when we get home tonight." I tipped my head to the left and scowled at her. "And what do you mean? Tell him what? I'm still not 100 percent convinced myself, so why should I tell him?"

Ears flapping, she shook her head before heading over to her big dog cushion to circle three times and lie down with a huff.

"Don't huff at me, Soph. I haven't decided if she did it or not."

But I really had. I was halfway, or there 'bouts, through the dissertation and I really had no doubts—well almost no doubts. I just didn't feel I could point the finger yet. Maybe it was Jebbin admitting they'd asked for the more thorough search. Let obnoxious Henry Schneider find the goods, or better, let Jason Anderson find it. Let Chatty or Antonia and her techs find whose stash it was. Then if I was wrong, I wouldn't look the fool again.

I set my plate on the kitchen table, myself in my chair, and picked up Dr. Garrow's—Cam's—paper. One thought kept niggling at me. I was taking the coward's way out.

CHAPTER 20

We were back where we started, in a way. Not totally, but Dr. Archibald Finlay Dawson had been murdered six nights ago after the opening dinner of the Midwest Anthropological Studies Society's Conference and now we sat at the conference's closing dinner. We were even sitting at a table in the same place in the room with the same seating arrangement. Naomi Malkoff was on my left and everyone else where they had been before, going around clockwise until you got to Jebbin on my right, with an empty chair between us.

The chair where Archie had been sitting that first night.

Resting in the center of his place setting were flowers that looked like a man's boutonnière. It certainly came from Aine's shop, as a hand-written tag was attached explaining that the forget-me-not was self-explanatory, the lemon balm meant sympathy, and the red poppy was for consolation. A nice gesture on someone's part.

I turned to Naomi. How differently I felt about her now. She was a nice young woman.

"Are you going back to Prairie Grass State College in the fall?"

"Hmm?" She looked at me, eyes startled wide. "Pardon?"

"Are you going back to Prairie Grass next fall?"

"Sorry, I was just remembering, you know. Last Friday. I haven't decided yet, Emory. Not so much that it won't be the same without

Dr. Dawson, more that I'm not sure what I want to do now." She frowned. "Maybe I need a break. It's been school for what? Eighteen years. I suddenly feel I want to do something else, for a while at least. You know, maybe a year in Europe or something like that."

She would pick Europe, wouldn't she? Was I losing Molly to Europe? She hadn't said much at all about missing home, and with what's-his-name . . . Freddy being English, he might try to talk her into doing her graduate work at a school over there.

"Emory?"

Naomi was staring at me.

"Sorry, I got distracted. A year off could be good. I usually don't think so for students going from high school to college, but it's different between college and grad school. I always feel it's more certain a person will go back and finish that masters. Although, I know with doctorates, there are a lot who never do their dissertations."

"True, but I'm not even sure I want the masters anymore. I worked at a florist shop my last two years of high school and I loved it. I took some botany classes my junior and senior years of college, and so I'm thinking I just might find a job at a flower shop. Give private cello lessons as well and save toward having my own flower shop."

She looked off into the future. I was sure she saw her shop, a charming display in the window, herself standing in the open doorway.

"I've decided I want to try to do what I love. I mean, I really like history and anthropology sounded interesting, but I love flowers and plants and beautiful music played on a cello. I think it will be a Victorian-looking shop and I'll help people pick out flowers that say what they want to say. You know, really use the meaning behind every flower."

"It sounds lovely!" Myra had been listening in.

"Excuse me," a voice behind me and to my right inquired. "Is this seat taken?"

It was Sonya, and the seat she wanted had been Archie's last Friday night.

Jebbin stood and pulled out the empty chair that had been between us.

"No, it isn't, please join us. You're Sonya Dawson, aren't you?"

She sat as Jebbin nudged the chair into place.

"Yes, and you're Emory's husband, I think." She smiled at him. "But I hope you'll forgive me, I don't remember your name."

"I'm Jebbin Crawford, and yes, Emory is my wife. I maybe should have told you before you sat down that this was your husband's chair at the opening dinner. I hope that doesn't bother you."

"No. Actually that's part of why I wanted to sit here. Sort of, well, I guess a strange part of saying goodbye to him." She picked up the boutonnière, gently touched the flowers, and then stuck it into her glass of water. "I spotted him here that night. But I've another reason as well." She waved her first reason aside with a graceful gesture. "I have friends at this table now: Emory, Naomi, and Myra, whom I remember fondly from when I used to come with Archie to the conference every year, and I wanted to be with them tonight."

Naomi, Myra, and I gratefully acknowledged the compliment, then Myra started reminiscing with Sonya. I decided to have a look at the program that sat at each person's place.

I leaned back in my chair and got Jebbin's attention.

"You're speaking?"

He looked heavenward and sighed. "Yes. I got here and Dr. Lindberg told me he put me in just before the programs were printed off this afternoon. I'm part of the "In Memory" part of the program and I'm supposed to say a few things about Dr. Archibald Finlay Dawson—fiddle player and bluegrass aficionado. I'm last to speak, my part is right before we play two of the four songs you picked out, so be sure you decide which two and you can let me know just before we go on."

"What about warming up? Are you going to have time?"

He shook his head. "No. I've moved my banjo onto a stack of unused chairs in the service hallway just to the side of the door to the right of the platform. You know, right side from the audience view."

"Oh, my fiddle is still in the dance classroom. Is that OK?"

The little warm-up room we'd used last Friday was locked tonight. I don't really like the dance room with all its, for me, eerie mirrors, but it was the next closest room to the meeting room where the dinner was being held. At least there was one corner with cupboards and no mirrors where I could warm up without watching myself warming up.

"That's fine, hon. You should get up when I do, walk with me as far as the step at the side of the stage, but just go out the door there instead. Keep an ear open, I'll do some tuning in the hall and you'll know it's time to go on."

"I will. But are you sure you'll need to tune?"

My dear man raised an eyebrow at me. "Ha. Ha. Ha."

I batted my lashes in return. It's a well-known fact, amongst those who play bluegrass, that no one tunes more often than the banjo player. For whatever reason, the silly things don't hold a tuning well. Especially the third string up from the bottom.

We would have said more but Dr. Charles A. Lindberg rose and headed for the podium to open the closing dinner of the Midwest Anthropological Studies Society's annual conference.

CHAPTER 21

I looked around as Dr. Lindberg spoke. There she was. Dr. Cameron Garrow, sitting just as she had before at the opening dinner, one row back from us and to my left.

She sat beside an empty chair like the one that had been at our table until Sonya Dawson sat there. Sitting next to Timothy Law's empty chair with the same boutonniere in the center of the place setting as had been at Archie's place. And she didn't even look awkward.

Cameron was dressed up more than usual tonight. She had on her sage-green, long, A-line dress, but this time she had a metallic yarn sweater the color of the inside of a butternut squash under it and a black lace shawl over her shoulders with beads or sequins on it that caught the light.

Like she was celebrating.

My jaws clenched as a hot flash rose that had nothing to do with being pre-menopausal. I could hardly wait to tell Jairus and the authorities. Yes, better have Jairus there or I'd catch all sorts of flack from Captain Schneider. That thought made me feel even more irate. Jebbin would stand by me though, he'd . . .

He'd do nothing but look surprised because I hadn't told him yet.

I looked around, but there weren't little notepads with the place settings this time. I dug into my smaller than usual purse and found nothing to write on there either. A mechanical pencil but no paper. I grabbed my program and wrote as small as I could, hoping no one else would be able to read it:

"*I've figured out the murderer. Have evidence to back it up. AnnaMay helped. It's Dr. Cameron Garrow. Will alert the powers that be after dinner is over.*"

I reached behind Sonya and tapped Jebbin's shoulder with the edge of the program, but the fabric of his jacket at the shoulder was too thick, so I tapped his neck. He reacted like a bug had got him, almost flicking the program out of my hand and onto the floor. When he looked around, I waved it in front of his face in a "take it, take it," manner. He took it and I mimed opening it, which he did. Even in profile I could see his eyes widen. He turned, about to speak, but I put my finger to my lips.

"Don't worry. All OK." I hoped he could read lips.

What are you getting into? His expression spoke clearly; like he'd caught one of our children with the lid off the cookie jar—hand poised to reach in, or a student just about to look at a crib note during a test.

Nothing. I'm fine. All's good, answered my exaggerated smile and casual flip of my hand.

He shook his head and looked back up at Dr. Lindberg, who was finishing his opening speech and about to announce that the buffet would begin.

Rapture.

Fiorello never failed to produce gastronomic rapture.

Loaves of his magical multigrain bread appeared on each table. Crescent rolls so light and airy they ought to have floated off the platters headed up the buffet tables next to buttery, layered, flakey biscuits kissed with honey. Then came a choice selection of leafy salads and pasta salads. Jebbin loves the Caesar salad and green peas salad, while I usually go for whatever the "choose your own dressing" leaf salad contains—a large variety of late spring/early summer lettuces this time—and Fio's special recipe honey-mustard dressing with shredded carrots, black olives, garbanzo beans, shredded cheese, and sliced purple onion added to the top. Oh, and the seafood salad with shell pasta, real scallops and real crabmeat. I really could make my whole meal with just that, but not when even more glorious things lay ahead.

Transport.

Bright orange, buttered baby carrots, ever so slightly sweet, as good as my mother's mom used to make. Broccoli and cauliflower florets that you can take with just their lightly seasoned butter sauce or add Fio's tangy, light cheese sauce that you pour on yourself to suit your tastes. I've seen Jebbin pour it over everything on his plate; it's that kind of good. Me, well I love the butter they're sautéed in. Can you ever have too much butter on veggies?

Exaltation.

Vegetarian lasagna and a lentil with swiss cheese casserole that are so scrumptious you don't even miss the meat. I know. I've had them before. Prime rib—need I say more—and inch-and-a-half-thick pork chops that are fork tender, seasoned with rosemary and white wine for the meat lovers. And, if there's room on your plate, a savory mix of wild brown and white rice and adorable little red skin potatoes all shiny with butter.

Heaven.

Heaven is thick, decadent cheesecake with top-it-yourself goodies to choose from. It's Death by Chocolate Cake, appropriately *not* labeled as such on this occasion. The luscious aroma of coffee and chocolate wafting from the tiramisu. The smiling wait staff with scoops in their hands ready to provide your choice of chocolate, vanilla, or strawberry ice cream for a sundae with all the fixins.

When we got back to our table, some member of the staff had taken the boutonnière out of Sonya's water glass and placed it in a bud vase. She reached out and touched the flowers, and a soft smile bloomed on her lips.

"He did have his moments, especially in our early years. Not all my memories are unhappy ones." She sat down, made the Greek Orthodox sign of the cross, and began to eat.

The sounds of conversation in the large room quieted as everyone savored their meals. When, after thirty minutes, a disembodied voice announced that the evening's program would begin in fifteen minutes, the ladies at our table, actually at most every table, followed our herd instinct and headed for the ladies room.

I ended up in line right behind Dr. Cameron Garrow.

She turned and smiled. "Well hello, Emory! I see you and Dr. Crawford are performing tonight."

I felt my face grow cold as my blood dropped from it to go wherever it goes when we turn pale. How could I just pleasantly chat with this woman? But something inside me said her time was nigh to hand, and I felt my confidence return along with my color.

"Yes, we are, but only two songs, not an entire performance."

"Murder songs to send the shining star of ethnomusicology on his way, since that's what placed him on the pedestal?"

My Lord! I could scarcely believe the woman's hutzpah! "Goodness no. That'd be rather out of place, don't you think? No. "Will the Circle be Unbroken" and "Finally Made It Home." Missing-someone-when-they're-gone songs."

Someone came out of a stall. It was Cameron's turn.

"It will be a memorable performance, I'm sure," she said over her shoulder.

Another stall became available and I locked myself in while wondering what her parting comment might mean. Now on edge and distracted, I went back to the banquet room, sat at our table, and fidgeted.

CHAPTER 22

Back at the table, we all listened to Dr. Emma Hodgkins and Dr. Robert Jones say a few things about their friend, Timothy Law. Then, Dr. Roy Gatlin, who taught in the anthropology department at Prairie Grass State College where Archie had been department head took the podium, the first to speak about Archie.

I wondered if everyone else could see how awkward it was for Dr. Gatlin, or was my intuition helping me pick up on it? He seemed to be struggling to find complimentary things to say about his newly-deceased superior. Jebbin would be next, and I'd have a chance to get out of here.

Why was I still feeling so antsy? It wasn't performance jitters. We'd done tons of performances and we'd done these two songs before in public. In a flash, I saw Jairus sitting across a picnic table from me in the soft glow of the security lights of Twombly College Observatory.

The gift.

OK. The gift was making me antsy.

So what was it trying to tell me?

"Emory."

My gift was saying my name.

"Emory, come on."

My husband was saying my name.

I got up and walked along with him to the edge of the stage. He went left up the steps to the platform and I went straight out the door to the service hall, turned right and down a-ways to the dance classroom.

Ugh! The endless reflections of the opposing walls of mirrors gave me vertigo as soon as I turned on the lights. There was something terrible there in that tunnel of wood floors, fluorescent lighting fixtures, and ballet barres. There always was something threatening down that infinite line of images, no matter where I met it, no matter what it reflected.

I tucked my head and scuttled into the corner with the cabinets like a beetle with a bird after it, opened my fiddle case, and focused on getting my fiddle and myself ready.

And that's why I didn't hear her.

"Turn around slowly or you'll die without answers an' I'd hate to disappoint you that way."

A gasp-yelp-gurgly sound came up from inside me.

Her and her darn Birkenstocks.

I slowly rotated, fiddle and bow in hand, to face Cameron. "Why . . . why slowly?"

Her gaze slid up and down me. "Dangerous things hold real still, then strike fast. Never trust quick movements. Though with you being shorter an' fatter than me, I'd bet good money on my bein' faster with my little stinger here."

She held a small pistol with a silencer on it.

"A gun?"

"I figured I wouldn't be able to get you to swallow any poison, and the topical ones just don't work fast enough."

"You're sounding southern." Lord, I was being brilliant.

"Aren't you just the most observant little thing? But, 'course that's what got ya into this mess. I was born and raised in the front range of the Blue Ridge Mountains in North Carolina. Not the first in my family to get a college degree—well for my dear brother it was an associates degree from a junior college, that counts, doesn't it? But I got my PhD. I got out of there and got a job teaching at a college while my brother and cousins are still back there scratchin' in the dirt."

I was closely watching her hand with the 'stinger' in it. Watching it glint, catching the light as she gestured with it. My brain left its wanderings to listen to her ramblings.

"You ought not to've got hold of my dissertation. You think you're the only one with friends at a library? My friend called me shortly after she sent it out. Suddenly thought it a small world sort of thing that the college I was at for the conference should happen to want my dissertation. And there you were, just cozyin' up to so many of us. I heard poor ole Timothy say he knew who did it while he was talking to you. He was the only one I knew of that had caught Archie and me working together. He found us together lookin' at research books in the stacks at Central Methodist University in Fayette, Missouri, where the conference was year before last. Didn't want to kill Tim. He was nice."

Her expression softened, the mother-earth, tree-hugging hippie showing through again.

"Yes, he was. I liked Timothy a lot."

She kept talking, which was what I wanted. Talking so she wouldn't hear what I saw in the mirrors. The motion caught my eye, even though I'd been doing my best to just look at Cameron and her metal stinger. With my peripheral vision, I saw several Jebbins come into the mirrored room. I thought, though I couldn't look long enough to be sure, that he was carrying his banjo by the neck. I didn't dare look that way, so I stared at Cameron's hands, which were waving about.

"I wanted to write a book," she was saying. "I wanted my family to see my name on a book at the library. See that I'd become someone important. Then the devil himself sidled up to me and whispered in my ear. 'You can write a book, Camie. I'll help you.

Write about music, folks like music and it'll sell to a bigger audience. You'll be a bestseller!' So I met the devil at a diner by a crossroads at midnight just outside of Emporia, Kansas where the MASS Conference was, four years ago. Just like the old superstitions, meet 'im at the crossroads. I sold my soul for a book and Archie Dawson took it all; my soul, my book, and my dreams."

Her eyes focused on mine, lit by a fire that looked like she had indeed sold her soul to a devil. She pointed at me with that shiny, deadly, little pistol. "You were stupid enough to risk your soul by figurin' it out an' now you're gonna pay with your soul."

"Stop, or I'll denature your proteins!" Jebbin's voice echoed in the large, mirrored room.

She hesitated, and that was all we needed. Wielding my bow like a fencing foil, I smacked her pistol hand away from me with a sharp thwack as the banjo came 'round in a two-handed swing upside Cameron's head. She went down as the body of Jebbin's one-of-a-kind Kat Eyz copper banjo parted from its neck and swayed like a pendulum by its strings.

CHAPTER 23

"Denature her proteins?"

The banquet was long over. Jairus, Chatty, Detective Jason Anderson, Sonya, Myra, Naomi, Jebbin and I were sitting around the only table still left in the room. Captain Henry Schneider paced around it asking questions.

"Denature her proteins?" Henry demanded again. "What the hell does that mean? I thought you hit her with that stupid banjo of yours."

"I did hit Cameron with the banjo. It seemed the better choice once I got in there." Jebbin grinned like a spelling-bee winner. "But I did have, well, still do have, a bottle of hydrochloric acid in my pocket. Dr. Chatterjee needed it for some tests he was running. Not sure how it ended up in my pocket."

"Yeah, yeah, whatever." Henry stopped pacing at the opposite side of the table so he could glare at Jebbin. "I'm sure all mad scientists carry the stuff around, but what does that have to do with the weird comment."

"Well, Captain Schneider, think of frying an egg. The white is actually clear until it starts getting hot, then it turns white. The yolk looks a different shade of yellow too after it starts cooking. Egg white and yolk are mostly protein, and the heat causes a specific damage to the shape of the proteins and that damage changes the physical properties of the substance the proteins are in. Acid does the same thing. It would have denatured the protein in her skin. In other words, it would have burned her skin. When I went into the hall to get my banjo and started tuning, Emory didn't come out of the classroom like we'd arranged. I knew she was in there 'cause the lights were on. I'd seen Cameron leave just after I took the stage, and I knew Emory suspected her, so I tippy-toed over to the room and I could see the two of them in the mirrors."

"She didn't see Jebbin because she had asked me to turn around. She was facing the cupboards," I put in.

"And you!" Henry turned on me. I should've kept my mouth shut. "You figured this out all by your little lonesome, huh?"

"Well . . . yes. Yes, I did. I had help from AnnaMay up in the library, but other than that just my gut feelings and thinking things through."

"Just don't go doing anything like this again, Mrs. Crawford. You got lucky this time. Almost got killed for it too. Just stay away from investigations from now on."

Henry nodded a goodbye to Jairus before stomping out. We all waited until we figured he was out of range, then burst out laughing.

Jason finally got his breath enough to talk. "We were all rather surprised when Dr. Garrow came to and gushed out that confession. She sure wasn't happy with you, Emory."

I leaned into my husband as he hugged me. "I guess all my years of reading paid off. I just knew Archie's book felt wrong, that the voice wasn't his." I looked at Jairus. "That and some good old fashioned 'feminine intuition.'"

Jebbin kissed the side of my head. "Guess you'll need to make room on the force for a new detective." He winked at Jason.

"Oh no." I snuggled closer and smiled at our friends around the table. "I'm keeping my amateur status. Just like Miss Jane Marple."

EPILOGUE

Sophie chased a squirrel into Fountain Garden and I followed with only the slightest twinge of apprehension. Autumn leaves floated on the late October breeze and danced with the streams of water before falling like the streams into the star-shaped pool. Just last weekend Jebbin and I, with his Kat Eyz banjo all fixed like new, had a small jam session in this garden with some of our friends. I gave a smile and a nod to Archie's spirit, wherever he was, as I'm sure he would have rather been jamming with us, even though none of us are big name bluegrass stars. Today, I spotted Naomi sitting on one of the benches around the fountain. She was deep in discussion with Aine McAllister and I chose not to disturb them. Twombly being the town it is, Aine had somehow found out that Naomi was considering becoming a florist with a Victorian love for the language of flowers and she immediately offered her an apprenticeship. Naomi says she is still going to get a masters in ethnomusicology and blend that knowledge into her flower shop. She'll sell flowers and plants along with classical and acoustic music. She's already chosen its name, Floral Melodies. The three of us have lunch every third Wednesday of the month.

My dog headed down the walkway that led home and I followed after, in no hurry to overtake her. Sophie'd be sitting on the porch smiling at me when I finally arrived.

As I headed up the steps of the front porch, in my mind I saw Myra Fordyce's dried flower arrangement in the disturbing black plastic bag and I smiled at the memory. The arrangement is on a bookshelf in our family room with a postcard from Myra leaning against it; a little note to let me know that she's at a Hutterite colony in Gibbon, Minnesota, this year. She heard from Sonya, who is well and getting married in the spring, in Greece.

I was content as I headed inside to get dinner going. It's Friday, and Molly and Freddy will be coming from Urbana for our regular dinner and a movie night.

END

Thank You

I wish to thank God for giving me the gift of creativity and for being able to turn words into stories.

Near the end of 2002, a writer of Tolkien-based fan fiction, pen name Shirebound, encouraged me to try my hand at writing fan fiction and post a story after I mentioned that I often made up stories about the hobbits Merry and Pippin. I wrote a story, posted it, and was pleasantly surprised at the many positive reviews it received. I wrote Tolkien fan fiction steadily from 2003 thru 2010, producing nearly 200 stories. Many of my regular readers began to encourage me to write a story of my own that could be published, and here it is. It wouldn't be here if not for those wonderful friends in the world of Tolkien fan fiction. Bless and thank you all.

My husband, daughter, and son have supported and encouraged me even though they had to deal with all my emotional ups and downs through the process of writing this book. They have been my solid fans with all the dreams I've ever chased and they, along with their spouses and kids, are the most important people in my life. I love you all dearly.

Sydell Voeller, my instructor for the "Breaking Into Print" course at Long Ridge Writers Group, helped with my early efforts at professional writing and recommended me for the school's novel writing course. She got this ball rolling. Hugs & thank you.

Mary Rosenblum. This wouldn't have happened without Mary. She has loved Emory and Jebbin and their story since she read a summary of it in my first lesson as her student in the "Write, Shape and Sell Your Novel" course at Long Ridge Writers Group. After I finished the course she became my writing coach. Her excitement and enthusiasm have kept me going and *Music can be Murder* wouldn't exist if I hadn't had her unfailing support. There is no version of 'thank you' that's enough to express my thanks to you, Mary. Love & hugs.

Fellow writer, photographer, artist, and dear friend Nancy Saul who did some editing and beta reading for me and gave me lots of all 'round encouragement. Love & Hugs.

Many thanks to Dr. Michael and Jennifer Ramm, who are both chemistry professors at Lincoln Land Community College in Springfield, Illinois, for a great deal of encouragement, inspiration, information, and friendship. Jennifer is also a professional bluegrass fiddler and the host of Bluegrass Breakdown on WUIS public radio 91.9 FM, Springfield, IL. Love ya, you're both awesome—and chemistry is cool!

My dear friends Vicki, Terry, Ginger, and Kelly. You are all in my book. I hope you enjoy finding yourselves and like the characters I made with inspirations from you. Love & hugs to you all.

ACKNOWLEDGEMENTS

Martin Brunkalla – luthier
Located 3 miles south of Marengo, IL
(No current contact information available)

In the story Dr. Archibald Finlay Dawson's
five-string fiddle was made by Martin Brunkalla.

Mike Smith – Kat Eyz banjos & banjo bridges and Snuffy Smith banjo bridges
Mechanicsburg, IL
http://www.kateyzbb.com/
1-217-364-4179 - kateyzbb@aol.com

In the story Dr. Jebbin Crawford's banjo is a
copper-plated, Cheetah model, Kat Eyz banjo.

Also by Pearl R. Meaker

The Can Be Mysteries

Music can be Murder

Death can be Hooked

Mysteries can be Buried

Slightly quirky, always creative, Pearl R. Meaker has been an artist and craftsperson her whole life. Although she's always had stories in her head, they didn't come out where others could read them until the advent of home computers with their ease of making corrections and moving bits around.

When not playing with her story ideas you can find Pearl reading all sorts of books, knitting or crocheting, doing other arts and crafts, bird watching and photographing nature. She also plays bluegrass fiddle along with her banjo-picking husband.

The books in the Can Be Mysteries Series are reminiscent of Agatha Christie's Miss Marple mysteries, which is why Pearl has chosen to characterize her stories as "Murder Genteel."

Find Pearl at her webpage: www.pearlrmeaker.com
and on Facebook: https://www.facebook.com/PearlRMeaker